Robert Greene's Friar Bacon and Friar Bungay: A Retelling

David Bruce

Published by David Bruce, 2022.

This is a work of fiction. Similarities to real people, places, or events are entirely coincidental.

ROBERT GREENE'S FRIAR BACON AND FRIAR BUNGAY: A RETELLING

First edition. July 9, 2022.

Copyright © 2022 David Bruce.

ISBN: 979-8201613617

Written by David Bruce.

Table of Contents

Dedication

Dedicated to My Uncle Reuben Saturday

When he was a young man, my mother's brother Reuben wanted to escape from poverty and lard sandwiches, so he tried to run away from it. He stole a car so he could drive up north where he hoped to find opportunity, but he got caught and ended up on a Georgia chain gang for several months. In a chain gang, prisoners are shackled every few feet by the ankles to a long length of chain to keep them from escaping. They work in the hot sun while shackled to the chain, and when they sleep, they are shackled to the bed. No freedom, hard work, hot sun, no pay, bad food, and some mean guards.

When my uncle got released from the chain gang, he hitchhiked up north. He did what a lot of people trying to escape from poverty do: He drifted. He drifted from town to town, seeking opportunity and not finding it. He worked when he could, but the jobs were temporary and low pay. My uncle slept rough often, and he was hungry often. Once, when he was completely broke and completely hungry, he saw a restaurant with a buffet and went inside and asked to speak to the manager. He said, "I am very hungry, I don't have any money, and I would appreciate it very much if you would give me any food that the restaurant is going to throw away. I will be happy to wait by the rear entrance until you are ready to throw away food."

The manager told him to sit down at a table, and then the manager went to the buffet, loaded a big plate high with food, and gave it to him free of charge.

One way out of poverty is to get a good job, and my uncle got out of poverty by getting a job working with sheet metal.

My uncle's work ethic helped him. His employer sent him to California to do some special sheet-metal work, and the people in California wanted to keep him there. They explained that their California employees liked to come to work late, leave early, and take many days off. It was difficult to get someone who would show up and do the work they were supposed to do and were paid to do.

My uncle was also good with money. He got married, bought a house, and raised six children. Each time he made a mortgage payment, he paid extra money so he could pay off the mortgage faster.

If there was a sale on food, he bought lots of it. For example, if there was a sale on peanut butter, two jars for the price of one, he would buy twelve jars and sometimes go back the next day and buy six more jars.

If you went in his pantry — a closet set aside to store food — you saw that it was packed with food. If you went in his kitchen, you saw that he had taken off the doors of the high cabinets in which he stored food so that he could see the food. If you went in his bedroom, you saw that he had all the regular bedroom furniture, but he also had lots of shelves he had installed. The shelves were loaded with things that he had bought on sale that he knew his family could use: food (of course), light bulbs, toothpaste, toilet paper, etc. His bedroom looked like a warehouse.

Once he made a bad purchase: he bought a case of baked beans. Beans are beans, but the sauce they came in can taste good or bad, and the sauce these beans came in tasted bad. His kids told him, "Dad, throw those beans away! They're awful!"

But when you grow up poor, you don't throw beans away. For a long time, whenever my uncle and his family ate baked beans, they ate a mixture of one can of good baked beans and one can of bad baked beans.

My uncle's kids never had to eat lard sandwiches.

***

The doing of good deeds is important. As a free person, you can choose to live your life as a good person or as a bad person. To be a good person, do good deeds. To be a bad person, do bad deeds. If you do good deeds, you will become good. If you do bad deeds, you will become bad. To become the person you want to be, act as if you already are that kind of person. Each of us chooses what kind of person we will become. To become a good person, do the things a good person does. To become a bad person, do the things a bad person does. The opportunity to take action to become the kind of person you want to be is yours.

Educate Yourself
Read Like A Wolf Eats
Be Excellent to Each Other
Books Then, Books Now, Books Forever

***

In this retelling, as in all my retellings, I have tried to make the work of literature accessible to modern readers who may lack some of the knowledge about mythology, religion, and history that the literary work's contemporary audience had.

Do you know a language other than English? If you do, I give you permission to translate this book, copyright your translation, publish or self-publish it, and keep all the royalties for yourself. (Do give me credit, of course, for the original retelling.)

I would like to see my retellings of classic literature used in schools, so I give permission to the country of Finland (and all other countries) to give copies of this book to all students forever. I also give permission to the state of Texas (and all other states) to give copies of this book to all students forever. I also give permission to all teachers to give copies of this book to all students forever.

Teachers need not actually teach my retellings. Teachers are welcome to give students copies of my eBooks as background material. For example, if they are teaching Homer's *Iliad* and *Odyssey*, teachers are welcome to give students copies of my *Virgil's* Aeneid: *A Retelling in Prose* and tell students, "Here's another ancient epic you may want to read in your spare time."

CAST OF CHARACTERS

MALE CHARACTERS

King Henry III of England. His family name is Plantagenet.

Prince Edward. Prince of Wales, his Son. Edward's nickname is Ned.

Ralph Simnell. The King's Jester, aka Fool.

Lacy. Earl of Lincoln. Friend of Prince Edward. In Scene 6, he is called the Earl of Lincolnshire. He is also sometimes called the Lincoln Earl. Lacy's first name is Edward, and his nickname is Ned.

Warren. Earl of Sussex. Friend of Prince Edward.

Ermsby. A Gentleman. Friend of Prince Edward. Ermsby's first name is Will. He is one of King Henry III's chamberlains.

Friar Bacon.

Miles. Friar Bacon's Poor Scholar.

Friar Bungay.

Emperor of Germany. Frederick II. He is the King of Germany and the Holy Roman Emperor.

King of Castile. Ferdinand III.

Jacques Vandermast. A German Magician.

Burden. Mason. Clement. Doctors of Oxford.

Lambert. A Gentleman. A Country Squire.

1st Scholar. Lambert's Son.

Serlsby. A Gentleman. A Country Squire.

2nd Scholar. Serlsby's Son.

Gamekeeper. Margaret's Father.

Thomas. A Clown, aka country boy.

Richard. A Clown, aka country boy.

FEMALE CHARACTERS

Princess Eleanor. Daughter to the King of Castile.

Margaret. The Gamekeeper's Daughter. Called the Fair Maiden of Fressingfield. Her nicknames are Peggy and Peg.

Hostess of The Bell Inn at Henley.

Joan. A Country Wench. Friend to Margaret, whom she sometimes calls Peggy.

SUPERNATURAL CHARACTERS

Voice of the **Brazen Head**. It is made of brass.

Spirit in the shape of *Hercules.*

A Devil.

MINOR CHARACTERS

Constable.

A Post-Messenger. Servant of Lacy, Earl of Lincoln.

Lords, Clowns, Gamekeeper's Friend, etc.

NOTA BENE

KING HENRY III: 1207-1272 (Reigned 1216-1272)

Son of King John, he reigned for 56 years. At the beginning of his reign, much of England was controlled by the French Prince Louis (later King Louis VIII), but at the end of his reign, England was controlled by the King of England.

He assumed the throne at the age of nine and remained King until his death. He was known for his piety, unsuccessful invasions of France, and extractions of money from Jews. In 1263, the baron Simon de Montfort seized power. In 1264, King Henry III was defeated and captured in the Battle of Lewes. Prince Edward escaped and in 1265, he defeated Simon de Montfort, who was killed in the Battle of Evesham, and freed his father, King Henry III.

KING EDWARD I: 1239-1307 (Reigned 1272-1307)

Edward Longshanks fought and defeated the Welsh chieftains, and he made his eldest son the Prince of Wales. He won victories against the Scots, and he brought the coronation stone from Scone to Westminster.

In this play, he is not yet the King of England; instead, he is Prince Edward — the Prince of Wales.

In this play, his friends sometimes call him "Ned," which is a nickname for "Edward."

OTHER NOTES

In this culture, a man of higher rank would use words such as "thee," "thy," "thine," and "thou" to refer to a servant. However, two close friends or a husband and wife could properly use "thee," "thy," "thine," and "thou" to refer to each other.

Words such as "you" and "your" were more formal and respectful.

In this society, the word "wench" is not necessarily negative. Often, it is used affectionately.

The title "sirrah" was used to refer to a male of lower status, such as a servant, than the speaker.

As a Jester, Ralph Simnell has much freedom of speech. He is permitted to tease and even insult Edward, Prince of Wales. He can call Prince Edward by the nickname "Ned" and use the familiar pronouns "thee," "thy," "thine," and "thou" to refer to him. He can even call him "sirrah." Jesters are also known as Fools.

Characters in this book call Brasenose College at the University of Oxford by the name "Brazen-nose."

The word "brazen" means "made of brass," according to the Oxford English Dictionary; however, some authorities say it means "made of brass or bronze." One such authority is at Brazenose College in Oxford: See Appendix A.

CHAPTER 1

Near the town of Fremingham, approximately 90 miles northeast of London, Prince Edward, who was melancholy, stood apart from Lacy, Warren, Ermsby, and Ralph Simnell. Lacy is the Earl of Lincoln, Warren is the Earl of Sussex, Ermsby is a gentleman, and Ralph Simnell is the Jester, aka Fool, of the royal family.

"Why does my lord look like a troubled sky when Heaven's bright shining Sun is shadowed and obscured by a fog?" Lacy asked about Prince Edward. "Just now we chased the deer, and through the clearings we outran with our horses the proud, tall, frolicsome bucks that swiftly ran before the teasers like the wind. Never before were the deer of merry Fressingfield so vigorously and successfully hunted by jolly friends. Nor have the farmers shared such fat and generously given venison since one hundred years before this day."

Fressingfield is a town about nine miles north of Fremingham. The teasers were hunting dogs that were trained to rouse the game.

The aristocratic hunters gave their game to the local citizens, who were not allowed to hunt without permission in the royal forests.

Lacy continued, "Nor have I seen my lord more frolicsome in the hunt, but now his mood has changed to melancholy."

"Prince Edward got to the gamekeeper's lodge and was cheerful in the lodge for awhile, drinking ale and milk in country cans," Warren said. "But for some reason, whether it was the country's sweet content, or else the bonny, pretty damsel who filled our drinking cups and who seemed so stately and dignified in her red clothing, or else a qualm that crossed his stomach then and made him nauseous, he immediately fell into his melancholy mood."

"Sirrah Ralph, what do you say about your master?" Ermsby asked the Jester. "Shall he all dejected and spiritless live melancholy like this?"

"Do you hear me, Ned?" Ralph the Jester asked Prince Edward, using a nickname.

Brooding, Prince Edward did not hear him.

Ralph the Jester said to the others, "Look and see if he will speak to me! He will not!"

"What did thou say to me, Fool?" Prince Edward asked.

"Please, tell me, Ned," Ralph the Jester said. "Are thou in love with the gamekeeper's daughter?"

"And if I am, so what?" Prince Edward replied.

"Why, then, sirrah, I'll teach thee how to deceive Love," Ralph the Jester answered.

"How, Ralph?"

"Indeed, Sirrah Ned, thou shall put on my cap and my coat and my dagger, and I will put on thy clothes and thy sword; and so thou shall be my Fool."

As a Jester, Ralph wore a cockscomb cap and carried a wooden dagger.

"And what is the point of this?" Prince Edward asked.

"Why, do this so that thou shall deceive and trick Love; for Love is such a proud rascal that he will never meddle with Fools or children," Ralph the Jester replied. "Isn't Ralph's counsel good, Ned?"

The god of love is Cupid.

"Tell me, Ned Lacy," Prince Edward said. "Did thou look closely at the maiden and see how lovely and lively she looked in her country clothing? A bonnier, prettier wench all Suffolk cannot yield — all Suffolk! Nay, all England has no maiden as lovely and lively as she."

Both Fremingham and Fressingfield are in the county of Suffolk.

"Sirrah Will Ermsby, Ned is deceived," Ralph the Jester said.

"Why, Ralph?"

"He says all England has no such equal to the gamekeeper's daughter, and I say, and I'll stand by my opinion, there is one better in the county of Warwickshire," Ralph the Jester said.

"How do thou prove that, Ralph?" Ermsby asked.

"Why, isn't the Abbot of Warwickshire a learned man and has read many books, and do thou think he hasn't more learning than thou to choose a bonny, pretty wench? Yes, I promise thee that he does, and I promise that by his whole grammar."

The Abbot of Warwickshire had studied Latin grammar as part of the education necessary for an Abbot. Part of his "education" also included how to choose a bonny, pretty wench — the word "wench" at this time was not necessarily negative. Being so learned, he knew much more about choosing — and chasing — wenches than Prince Edward. After all, he has studied books,

and women are necessary parts of the Book of Love, and especially of the hole
— vagina — grammar.

"You reason well, Ralph," Ermsby said.

"I tell thee, Lacy, that her sparkling eyes flash forth sweet love's alluring fire,"
Prince Edward said, "and in her locks and tresses she enfolds the looks of those
who gaze upon her golden hair.

"Luna the Moon's bashful, modest white, mixed with the morning's red
of the dawn, is boastfully displayed on her lovely cheeks. Her face is Beauty's
tablet, where she paints the glories of her gorgeous excellence. Her teeth are like
underwater banks of precious margarites, aka pearls, richly enclosed with lips
like ruddy-red coral cliffs.

"Tush, Lacy, she is more beautiful than Beauty herself. Thou would know
this if thou would closely look at her exquisite features."

"I grant, my lord, that the damsel is as fair as humble Suffolk's homely
towns can yield," Lacy replied. "But in the court are more elegant dames than
she. These dames' faces are enriched with the tint and mark of noble birth,
their beauties stand upon the stage of fame, and they boast about their love
conquests in the Courts of Love."

The judges of a Court of Love were upper-class women who were either
married or widowed; they did such things as resolve disputes between lovers
and answer questions about courtly love.

"Ah, Ned, but if thou had watched her as I myself have," Prince Edward
said, "and seen the secret beauties of the maiden, then you would know that the
courtly coyness of the elegant ladies at court are only foolery and coquetry."

The gamekeeper's daughter's "secret beauties" could be beauties of character
and personality or those beauties that lie under her clothes.

"Why, how did you watch her, my lord?" Ermsby asked.

"When she moved like Venus, goddess of Beauty, through the house, and
her shape immediately engaged my thoughts, into the dairy I went with the
maiden," Prince Edward said, "and there among the cream-bowls she shone like
Pallas Athena, goddess of domestic skills, among her noble domestic tasks. She
pushed and twisted — to prevent slippage — the sleeves of her smock up her
lily-white arms, and dived them into milk to curdle her cheese."

By "smock," Prince Edward meant "dress." In this society, a smock is usually a woman's undergarment, so he may have been unconsciously — or consciously — thinking about her smock being moved to reveal the skin underneath.

He continued, "But her crystal skin, whiter than the milk and marked with the lines of azure-blue veins, made blush any woman whose beauty — whether created by the art of makeup or by nature — was brought for comparison to her.

"Ermsby, if thou had seen, as I did note well, how beauty played the housewife, how this girl, like Lucrece, laid her fingers to the work, thou would, with Tarquin, risk Rome and all else to win the lovely maiden of Fressingfield."

Lucrece, a Roman noblewoman, was a dutiful wife. While away from their homes, her husband and the sons of the King of Rome debated about who had the most virtuous wife. They decided to return to Rome and visit their wives late at night. The other wives were feasting, but Lucrece was spinning alongside her female servants.

Unfortunately, Sextus Tarquinius, son of King Tarquinius Superbus, later raped Lucrece. She committed suicide, and her brother led a rebellion that cast out King Tarquinius Superbus, who was the last King of the Romans.

"Sirrah Ned, would you like to have her?" Ralph Simnell asked.

"Aye, Ralph," Prince Edward replied.

"Why, Ned, I have formed a plot in my head; thou shall have her at once."

"I'll give thee a new coat if you can teach me how to have her."

"Why, Sirrah Ned, we'll ride to Oxford to see Friar Bacon," Ralph the Jester replied. "Oh, he is a splendid scholar, sirrah; they say that he is such a splendid necromancer and magician that he can make devils take the shape of women, and he can transform cats into apple-sellers."

"And what then, Ralph?"

"Indeed, sirrah, thou shall go to him, and so that thy father Harry the Third shall not miss thee, Friar Bacon shall turn me into thee; and I'll go to the court, and I'll prince it out," Ralph the Jester said. "And Friar Bacon shall turn thee into either a silken purse full of gold, or else a finely made lady's petticoat."

"But how shall I have the maiden?" Prince Edward asked.

"Indeed, sirrah, if thou should be transformed into a silken purse full of gold, then on Sundays she'll hang thee by her side, and you must not say a word. Now, sir, when she comes into a great crowd of people, for fear of the cutpurse, all of a sudden she'll stash thee beneath her petticoat; then, sirrah, being there, you may plead for yourself and take it from there."

In this culture, people carried money in bags, called purses, outside their clothing. A cutpurse would cut the string attaching the purse to the person whose money it was and steal the purse.

"That's an excellent scheme!" Ermsby said.

"But what if I should be transformed into a finely embroidered petticoat?"

"Then she'll put thee into her chest and lay thee onto lavender for later use, and on some good day she'll put thee on; and at night when you go to bed, then being turned from a petticoat to a man, you may get engaged to be married."

"Wonderfully wisely counseled, Ralph," Lacy said.

"Ralph shall have a new coat," Prince Edward promised.

"May God thank you when I have it on my back, Ned," Ralph the Jester said.

Prince Edward said, "Lacy, the Fool has laid a perfect plot because our country-girl Margaret is so shy and insists so much upon her principles of chastity and correct conduct that it's either marriage or no market — no sex — with the maiden."

He then said, "Ermsby, it must be necromantic spells and charms of the occult that must enchain her love, or else Edward shall never win the girl. Therefore, my merry lads, we'll mount our horses in the morning, and posthaste ride to Oxford to this jolly friar. Bacon shall by his magic do this deed."

"Good plan, my lord," Warren said, "and that's a speedy way to wean these headstrong puppies from the teat."

In other words, it's a quick way to convince chaste maidens to stop being chaste maidens.

"I am unknown and not recognized as the prince," Prince Edward said. "They think that we are only merry courtiers of the court, we who revel thus among our liege's game."

Prince Edward and his companions had been incognito during their visit to this place in the country. This would help him to bed the gamekeeper's daughter because members of royalty had to marry other members of royalty. Not knowing who Prince Edward was, Margaret the gamekeeper's daughter was likely to be more willing to bed him, especially if he promised — unfortunately, falsely — to marry her.

Prince Edward continued, "Therefore I have devised a stratagem.

"Lacy, thou know that next Friday is July 25, the feast day of Saint James the Greater. At that time the country citizens flock to the fair at nearby Harleston. Then the gamekeeper's daughter will enjoy herself there, and outshine the troop of all the maidens who come to see and to be seen that day.

"Disguised, you shall frequently go among the country-yokels. Disguise yourself as a farmer's son who lives not far from there.

"Spy out those who court her, and whom she likes best. Surpass him, and court her to control the clownish local yokel.

"Say that the courtier who was dressed all in green, and who helped her skillfully to curdle her cheese and who filled her father's lodge with venison, sends her his regards, and sends fairings — gifts from the fair — to herself.

"Buy something worthy of her commoner parentage. Don't attempt to buy something worthy of her beauty; for, Lacy, the fair offers for sale no jewel suitable for the maiden.

"And when thou talk about me, notice if she blushes. Oh, if she blushes, then she loves me; but if her cheeks grow pale, she feels disdain for me.

"Lacy, send me news about how she fares, and spare no time nor cost to win her love."

"I will, my lord, execute this responsibility as if I, Lacy, were in love with her."

"Send letters speedily to Oxford to give me the news," Prince Edward said.

"And, Sirrah Lacy, buy me a thousand thousand million of fine bells," Ralph the Jester said.

"What will thou do with them, Ralph?" Lacy asked.

"Indeed, every time that Ned sighs for the gamekeeper's daughter, I'll tie a bell about him: and so within three or four days I will send word to his father, Harry, that his son — my master Ned — has become Love's morris-dancer."

Morris-dancers often wore bells as they danced at festivals.

"Well, Lacy, carry out your responsibilities carefully, and I will hasten to Oxford to the friar, so that he by his occult art and thou by secret gifts to the gamekeeper's daughter may make me lord of merry Fressingfield," Prince Edward said.

"May God send your honor your heart's desire," Lacy said.

CHAPTER 2

— Scene 2 —

In Friar Bacon's cell — his living space — at Brasenose College at the University of Oxford, Friar Bacon, Miles, Burden, Mason, and Clement met. Miles was Friar Bacon's poor — in more ways than one — student who earned free tuition as well as room and board by working as Friar Bacon's servant; he was holding books under his arm. Burden, Mason, and Clement were academic doctors and heads of their colleges at Oxford.

"Miles, where are you?" Friar Bacon called.

"*Hic sum, doctissime et reverendissime doctor*," Miles replied.

Miles' Latin was often imperfect, but it was usually understandable. Here he was saying, "Here I am, most learned and most reverend doctor."

Friar Bacon asked, "*Attulisti nos libros meos de necromantia?*"

[Friar Bacon asked, "Have you brought us our books on necromancy?"]

Miles replied, "*Ecce quam bonum et quam jucundum habitare libros in unum!*"

[Miles replied, "Behold, how good and how pleasant it is for books to dwell together in unity!"]

Psalm 133:1 states, "*Behold, how good and how pleasant it is for brethren to dwell together in unity!*" (King James Bible).

Friar Bacon asked, "Now, masters of our academic state who rule in Oxford as viceroys of your college, and whose heads contain maps of the liberal arts, spending your time in the depths of learned skill, why do you thus flock to the secluded cell of Bacon, a friar newly installed in Brazen-nose?"

"Brazen-nose" was a nickname for Brasenose. At Brasenose was a brass doorknocker in the form of a lion's head with a large nose.

Friar Bacon's visitors were very important. As viceroys, they were heads of their colleges at Oxford. Their heads also contained "maps of the liberal arts" — in other words, they were experts in the liberal arts.

In the Middle Ages, seven classical areas of academic study made up the liberal arts. They were divided into the *trivium* and the *quadrium*. The *trivium* consisted of grammar, logic, and rhetoric, and the *quadrium* consisted of arithmetic, geometry, astronomy, and music.

Friar Bacon continued, "Say what's on your mind, so that I may make a reply."

"Bacon, we have heard something that we long have suspected — that thou have studied magic's mystery," Burden said. "You have learned from pyromancy how to divine by flames. You have learned to foretell the future by the use of hydromancy and the study of ebbs and tides."

Hydromancy used observations of water to foretell the future.

Burden continued, "You have learned to use aeromancy to answer difficult questions, as the god Apollo did."

Aeromancy used observations of atmospheric phenomena to foretell the future.

The Delphic Oracle was a priestess of Apollo, god of prophecy. People in the ancient world traveled to her to receive answers to their difficult questions, answers that were given to her by Apollo.

In this culture, people believed that the four elements that made up the entire universe could be used in divination. The Oxford doctors had mentioned three: 1) fire and pyromancy, 2) water and hydromancy, and 3) air and aeromancy. They did not mention earth and geomancy.

"Well, Master Burden, what about all this?" Friar Bacon asked.

"Indeed, sir," Miles said, "he only fulfills, by rehearsing of these names, the moral of the fable of the Fox and the Grapes: That which is above us pertains not at all to us."

Aesop's fable of the Fox and the Grapes is about a fox that wishes to eat some grapes but cannot reach them. As the Fox leaves, he says, "I bet those grapes were sour, anyway."

Miles' point is that just as the grapes are above the fox and out of reach, so the occult arts are above and out of reach of the visiting Oxford doctors.

"I tell thee, Bacon, rumors at Oxford say — actually, all England, and the court of Henry says — that thou are making a Brass Head by the use of magic, a Head that shall explain strange mysteries and speak true principles and instruct you in philosophy," Burden said. "Rumors also say that with the help of devils and ghastly, terrible fiends, thou intend, before many years or days have passed, to surround England with a wall of brass."

"And what about this?" Friar Bacon asked.

"What about this, master!" Miles said. "Why, he speaks mystically."

"Mystically" was possibly a malapropism for "metaphorically" or "figuratively," but Burden was speaking literally about magic. However, the word "book" would soon be used figuratively.

Miles continued, "He knows that if your skill should fail to make a Brass Head, yet Mother Water's strong ale will suit his purpose to make him have a copper nose."

Copper is reddish, and so is a drunkard's nose.

In this culture, alkalized water was known as mother-water. It was an ingredient used to make copper-sulfate, which was also called copperas or vitriol. Copper-sulfate was used in dyeing and tanning.

"Bacon, we are not troubled by thy skill," Clement said. "Instead, we rejoice that our academy yields a man who is regarded as the wonder of the world. For if thy cunning should work these miracles, England and Europe shall marvel at thy reputation, and Oxford shall in letters of brass and statues, such as were built up in Rome, immortalize Friar Bacon for his magic."

"So then, gentle friar," Mason said, "tell us what you intend to do."

"Seeing that you have come as friends to me, the friar, know, doctors, that I, Friar Bacon, can by use of my knowledge gained from my books make Boreas — the north wind — thunder from his cave, and I can make fair Luna the Moon dim to a dark eclipse."

In mythology, the winds are imprisoned in a cave until Aeolus, god of the winds, lets them loose.

Friar Bacon continued, "The great arch-ruler, who is the potentate of Hell, trembles when Bacon bids him, or his fiends, to bow to and submit to the force of his pentagram. What magic can work, the frolicsome friar knows; and therefore I will turn to my magic book and strain out necromancy to the deep — I will learn magic to the greatest extent I can.

"I have invented and created a Head of Brass — I made Belcephon, a demon who serves me, hammer out the stuff. That Head of Brass by magic shall teach me philosophy. I will strengthen England by creating a wall of brass with my skill, so that even if ten Caesars were to live and reign in Rome, along with all the legions Europe contains, they would not touch a blade of grass of English ground. The work that Ninus reared at Babylon, the brass walls created by Semiramis, which were carved to resemble the gateway of the Sun-god, shall not be such as will ring the English shore from Dover to the marketplace of Rye."

Ninus founded Babylon, and his wife, Semiramis, ordered the walls of Babylon to be built.

"Is this possible?" Burden asked.

"I'll bring you two or three witnesses," Miles said.

"Who are those witnesses?" Burden asked.

"Indeed, sir, three or four are as honest devils and good companions as any are in Hell," Miles said.

"There is no doubt that magic may do much in this," Mason said, "For he who studies the principles of mathematics, astronomy, and astrology will find precepts that will help him to work wonders that surpass the common perception and ordinary understanding of men."

"But Bacon shoots a bow and tries to reach a distance that is beyond his ability to achieve — he is promising more than he can deliver," Burden objected. "He tells us more than magic can perform, thinking to gain fame by such foolishness.

"Haven't I gotten as far as Bacon in the achievement of academic degrees and honors, and haven't I studied many secrets? Yet to think that Heads of Brass can utter any voice, or more, to talk about deep philosophy — well, this is a fable Aesop had forgotten."

In other words, such a tale is too bizarre even for Aesop.

"Burden, thou wrong me when thou disparage me like this," Friar Bacon said. "Bacon loves not to stuff himself with lies. But answer me in front of these doctors, if thou dare, certain questions I shall ask thee."

"I will," Burden said. "Ask what thou can."

"Indeed, sir, he'll immediately be on you piggyback to know whether the feminine or the masculine gender in Latin is most worthy," Miles said.

William Lily wrote a Latin grammar in which he claimed that the masculine gender is more worthy than the feminine gender, and that the feminine gender is more worthy than the neuter. Some Latin word endings are masculine, some are feminine, and some are neuter.

"Weren't you yesterday, Master Burden, at Henley upon the Thames?" Friar Bacon asked.

"I was," Burden answered. "What about it?"

"What book did you study thereon all night?"

"I! None at all," Burden said. "I read there not even a line."

"If that is true, doctors, then Friar Bacon's magic knows nothing," Friar Bacon said.

Friar Bacon definitely thought his magic knew something — he was asserting that Burden had read a book, or "book" — in Henley.

"What do you say to this, Master Burden?" Clement said. "Doesn't he touch you? Hasn't he struck a nerve?"

"I don't care about his frivolous speeches," Burden said.

"Nay, Master Burden, before my master has finished with you, he will turn you from a doctor to a dunce, and shake you so small that he will leave no more learning in you than is in Balaam's ass," Miles said.

Balaam's ass was given speech by an angel and so it was remarkably well educated for an ass, but a well-educated ass is no match for a well-educated scholar.

"Masters, because learned Burden's skill is deep, and because he intensely doubts Bacon's cabalistic — secret and esoteric — skills in the occult, I'll show you why he often travels to Henley," Friar Bacon said. "He goes to Henley, doctors, not in order to smell the fragrant air, but to spend the night there in alchemy, to multiply — transform base metal into precious gold or silver — with secret spells of magic. Thus secretly he steals learning from us all. To prove that what I say is true, I'll show you immediately the book he keeps at Henley for himself."

"Now that my master goes to conjuring, take heed," Miles said.

The scholars were frightened. Conjuring often involved summoning devils.

"Masters, stand still, and don't be afraid," Friar Bacon said. "I'll show you only his book."

He then conjured, "*Per omnes deos infernales, Belcephon!*"

[He then conjured, "By all the infernal deities, Belcephon!"]

A hostess of an inn magically appeared with a shoulder of mutton on a spit, and a devil — Belcephon — appeared.

Burden had not been studying a literal book, but instead a figurative book. This "book" was a woman. A book needs a cover, and Burden had been covering her — getting on top of her — in bed.

"Oh, master, cease your conjuration, or you will spoil everything," Miles said, "for here's a she-devil come with a shoulder of mutton on a spit. You have marred the devil's supper, but no doubt he thinks our college food is meager, and so he has sent you his cook with a shoulder of mutton, to increase the amount of food for us to eat."

In this culture, the word "mutton" was slang for a prostitute. Guess what the spitted mutton symbolized.

"Oh, where am I?" the hostess asked. "What's become of me?"

"Who are thou?" Friar Bacon asked.

"I am the hostess at Henley; I am the mistress of the Bell Inn."

"How came thou to be here?" Friar Bacon asked.

"As I was in the kitchen among the maids, spitting the meat to make supper for my guests, an impulse moved me to look out of doors," the hostess said. "No sooner had I peered into the yard but immediately a whirlwind hoisted me from there, and mounted me aloft into the clouds. As if I were in a trance, I neither thought nor feared anything. Neither do I know where or whither I was taken, nor where I am nor who these people are."

"No?" Friar Bacon asked. "Don't you know Master Burden?"

"Oh, yes, good sir, he is my daily guest," the hostess replied.

She then said, "What, Master Burden! It was only yesterday night that you and I at Henley played at cards."

Earlier, Bacon said that Burden spent time at Henley multiplying. Apparently, a game of cards is not all the hostess and Burden were playing.

"I don't know what we did," Burden said.

He cursed, "A pox on all conjuring friars!"

"Now, jolly friar," Clement said to Friar Bacon, "tell us, is this the 'book' that Burden is so careful to look on?"

"It is," Friar Bacon answered.

He then said, "But, Burden, tell me, do thou now believe that Bacon's necromantic skill cannot create his Brazen Head and wall of brass, when he can fetch thine hostess so quickly!"

Miles said, "I'll assure you, master, if Master Burden could conjure as well as you, he would have his book every night come from Henley for him to study on at Oxford."

The "book" he would "study" on each night would be the hostess.

Mason asked, "Burden, are you checkmated by this frolicsome friar?"

He then said to the others, "Look how he droops; his guilty conscience drives him to bashfulness and makes his hostess blush."

"Well, mistress, because I will not have you missed, you shall return to Henley to cheer up your guests before supper begins," Friar Bacon said to the hostess.

He then said, "Burden, bid her adieu; say farewell to your hostess before she goes."

He then ordered Belcephon the devil, "Sirrah, leave, and set her safely at home."

"Master Burden, when shall we see you at Henley?" the hostess asked.

"May the devil take thee and Henley, too!" Burden said.

The hostess and the devil exited.

"Master, shall I make a good suggestion?" Miles asked.

"What is it?" Friar Bacon asked.

"Indeed, sir, now that the hostess has gone to provide supper for her customers, conjure up another spirit, and send Doctor Burden flying after her."

Ignoring the suggestion, Friar Bacon said to the others, "Thus, rulers of our academic state, you have seen the friar — me — demonstrate and thereby prove that his magic is real. And as the college called Brazen-nose is under him, and he is the master there, so surely shall this Head of Brass be created and state strange and unknown truths. And Hell and Hecate shall fail the friar, but I will surround England with a brass wall."

Friar Bacon may have said "An" ["If"] instead of "And," and so this last sentence was ambiguous. It could mean:

1) And Hell and Hecate shall fail me, the friar, but I will surround England with a brass wall.

2) Even if Hell and Hecate shall fail me, the friar, I will surround England with a brass wall.

Events would show that Friar Bacon should have said this:

3) Unless Hell and Hecate shall fail me, the friar, I will surround England with a brass wall.

Miles said, "So be it *et nunc et semper*. Amen."

[Miles said, "So be it both now and always. Amen."]

The phrase "both now and always" was taken from the doxology (a short hymn of praise) titled "*Gloria Patri.*" "*Sicut erat in principio et nunc et semper, et in saecula aeculorum. Amen*" means "As it was in the beginning, and now, and ever shall be, world without end. Amen."

CHAPTER 3

— Scene 3 —

At the Harleston Fair, Margaret the gamekeeper's daughter talked with her friend Joan and the country boys Thomas and Richard. Other country folk were present, as was Lacy, who was disguised in country apparel. He was pretending to be a farmer's son.

"I swear, Margaret," Thomas said, "here's a weather that is able to make a man call his father 'whoreson.' If this good weather continues, we shall have such plentiful crops that hay will be sold at a cheap price, and butter and cheese at Harleston will bear no price — they will have no financial value."

Good weather meant plentiful crops, which meant low prices. This had both positives and negatives. Plentiful crops meant lots of food for the winter, but low prices were good for the buyer but bad for the seller. If a man were a buyer, he might call his father "whoreson" in a friendly, joking way, but if a man were a seller and his father sets the prices for what he sold, he might be angry and insult his father by calling him "whoreson."

"Thomas, when maidens come to see the fair, they don't come to make a bargain for a dearth of hay," Margaret said. "When we have salted our butter and set our cheese safely upon the racks, then we let our fathers price it as they please.

"We country sluts of merry Fressingfield come to the fair to buy needless naughts — unnecessary things — to make us look attractive."

She was using the word "sluts" in a playful way — in this case, the word really meant "young women" or perhaps "kitchen-maids."

She added, "And we look to see that young men should be generous this day, and court us with such fairings — gifts bought at the fair — as they can afford.

"Today Phoebus Apollo the Sun-god is joyous, and playfully looks down from Heaven, as when he courted lovely Semele."

Actually, it was Jupiter who courted Semele. She insisted that she be allowed to see the god in all his glory. When Jupiter allowed her to do this, the sight burned her to ashes.

On this fair Harleston Fair day, the Sun was shining brightly, but it was not shining as brightly as Jupiter did when he revealed himself in all his glory to Semele.

Margaret continued, "Phoebus Apollo swears that the peddlers shall have empty packs if it is true that fair weather may make merchants buy."

If the merchants made money as they likely would if fair weather encouraged lots of people to attend the fair, they would spend some of that money on the items the peddlers sold.

"But, lovely Peggy," the disguised Lacy said, "Semele is dead, and therefore Phoebus from his palace looks, and seeing such a sweet and attractive saint as you, shows all his glories in order to court you."

Despite his good education, Lacy did not correct Margaret's mistake about who had courted Semele. It is not a good idea to correct a woman you are courting.

"This is a fair-gift, gentle sir, indeed, to tease me with such smooth flattery," Margaret said. "But learn this from me: Your teasing of me is too obvious."

She then said, "Well, Joan, our beauties must put up with their jests. We serve this purpose in jolly Fressingfield."

Joan, whose purpose was to find a husband at the fair, said, "Margaret, a farmer's daughter for a farmer's son. I assure you that the meanest of us two shall have a mate to lead us from the church."

The disguised Lacy whispered to Margaret in her ear.

"But, Thomas, what's the news?" Joan said. "What, down in the dumps? Give me your hand. We are near a peddler's shop. Out with your purse — we must have fair-gifts now."

"Indeed, Joan, and you shall," Thomas said. "I'll bestow a fair-gift on you, and then we will go to the tavern, and snap off a pint of wine or two."

Margaret asked the disguised Lacy, "Where do you come from, sir? Are you from Suffolk? I ask because your words and expressions are finer than those of the common sort of men."

As a courtier, Lacy was much better educated than farmers and farmers' sons — and farmers' daughters.

"Indeed, lovely girl, I am from near Beccles," Lacy said, naming a town just far enough away that Margaret would not grow suspicious because no one knew him. "I am your neighbor, not more than six miles away from here, a farmer's son, who never was so odd that he could not be courteous to such dames as you. But trust me, Margaret, I am sent with a specific duty to perform from that man who reveled in your father's house, and who, wearing green, filled your father's lodge with cheer and venison. He has sent you this purse rich with money; this is his token that he helped you curdle your cheese and chatted with you in the dairy."

"To me?" Margaret asked.

She meant, *He sent this purse of money to me?* But Lacy thought she was asking, *He talked to me?*

"You have forgotten," the disguised Lacy said. "Women are often weak in memory."

"Oh, pardon me, sir," Margaret said. "I remember the man. It would be impolite to refuse his gift, and yet I hope he sends it not out of love because we have little leisure to debate about that."

"What, Margaret!" Joan said. "Don't blush! Maidens must have men who love them."

"Nay," Thomas said. "I swear by the mass that she looks pale as if she were angry."

"Sirrah, are you from Beccles?" Richard asked the disguised Lacy. "Please, tell me how is Goodman Cob? My father bought a horse from him."

"Goodman" was a title for a person, such as a farmer, whose rank was less than that of gentleman.

Richard then said, "I'll tell you, Margaret, that horse would be good as a gentleman's jade because — of all things — the foul hilding could not endure pulling a dung-cart."

Jades and hildings are bad horses. The horse that Richard's father had bought from Goodman Cob was not good for such farm tasks as pulling a cart filled with manure.

Margaret thought about the disguised Lacy, *How different this farmer is from the rest who until now have pleased my wandering sight! His words are witty and quickened with a smile. His manners are gentle, and he smells of the court. He is genial, and all his movements are debonair. He is proportioned as was Paris, Prince of Troy, when, dressed in the grey clothing of a shepherd, he courted the nymph Oenone in the river valley near Troy.*

Paris married Oenone, but he left her in order to go to Sparta and take Helen, who became Helen of Troy, away from her husband, King Menelaus of Sparta.

Margaret continued thinking, *Great lords have come and pleaded for my love: Who am I but the gamekeeper's lass of Fressingfield? And yet I think that this farmer's jolly son surpasses the most attractive man who has pleased my eye. But, Peg, disclose not that thou are in love, and show as yet no sign of love to him, although thou well would wish him to be thy love. Keep that to yourself until the right time comes to show the grief — the pain caused by love — with which thy heart does burn.*

Margaret then said out loud, "Come, Joan and Thomas, shall we go enjoy the fair?

"You, Beccles man, you will not abandon us now, I hope."

"Not while I may have the company of such attractive girls as you," the disguised Lacy said.

"Well, if you happen to come by Fressingfield, make just a step into the gamekeeper's lodge, and such poor fare as woodmen can afford — butter and cheese, cream and fat venison — you shall have plenty, and a welcome besides."

"Gramercies, Peggy," the disguised Lacy said. "Look for me before long."

"Gramercies" means "thank you very much." It is derived from the French "*grande merci*," which means "much thanks."

CHAPTER 4

At the Court at Hampton House, King Henry III, the Emperor of Germany, the King of Castile, Princess Eleanor (the King of Castile's daughter), and the German magician Jacques Vandermast talked together.

King Henry III said, "Great men of Europe, monarchs of the west, ringed with the walls of old Ocean, whose high surging waves are like the parapets on the top of the walls that surrounded high-built Babel with towers, welcome, my lords."

He was saying that the great river Ocean surrounded the known world. King Henry III's time was before that of Christopher Columbus, and so people knew nothing about the Americas.

King Henry III continued, "Welcome, splendid western kings, to England's shore, whose promontory-cliffs along the shore show that Albion — Britain — is another little world. English Henry says welcome to you all, and chiefly to the lovely Eleanor, who dared for Prince Edward's sake to cut through the seas and venture as Agenor's damsel did through the deep to get the love of Henry's amorous son."

Europa was the daughter of Agenor, King of Phoenicia. Jupiter fell in love with her, and after transforming into a majestic bull, he appeared to her. She climbed on his back, and he swam to Crete with her.

The King of Castile said to King Henry III, "England's rich monarch, brave Plantagenet, the Pyrenees Mountains that swelling above the clouds defend the wealthy Castile with walls could not detain the beauteous Eleanor."

King Henry III's father, King Henry II, was the first Plantagenet king.

The King of Castile continued, "Hearing of the fame of Prince Edward's youth, she dared to brook the sea-god Neptune's haughty pride and cross the waves, and endure the brunt of the perverse wind-god Aeolus and his adverse winds. May fair England welcome her all the more for these reasons."

Eleanor said, "After the English Henry the Third by his lords had sent Prince Edward's lovely portrait as a present to the Castile Eleanor, this attractive portrait of so splendid a man, and the virtuous fame given to his deeds of valor — and to Edward's courageous and steadfast determination —

done at the Holy Land before Damascus' walls, led both my eye and thoughts equally to like the English monarch's son so much that I braved great perils for his gratification."

"Where is Prince Edward, my lord?" the German Emperor asked.

King Henry III replied, "He traveled by horse, not long ago, from the court, to the border of the county of Suffolk, to merry Fremingham, in order to entertain himself among my brownish deer. From thence, by letters sent to Hampton House, we hear that the Prince has ridden with his lords to Oxford to hear debates among the learned men in the academy there. But we will send letters to my son to tell him to come from Oxford to the court."

The German Emperor said, "Nay, rather, Henry, let us, as we are, ride to visit Oxford with our train of attendants. I am eager to see your universities and what learned men your academy yields. From Hapsburg I have brought a learned scholar to hold a debate with English orators.

"This doctor, surnamed Jacques Vandermast, a German born, has traveled to Padua, to Florence, and to fair Bologna, to Paris, Rheims, and stately Orleans, and, talking there with men of the occult arts, he defeated the chiefest of them all in aphorisms, in magic, and in the mathematical rules of astronomy and astrology. Now let us, Henry, test him in your schools."

"He shall, my lord," King Henry III said. "I well like this proposal of yours. We'll progress immediately to Oxford with our trains of attendants and see what men our academy brings."

He then said, "And, wondrous Vandermast, welcome to me. In Oxford thou shall find a jolly friar called Friar Bacon, England's only flower. Make him nonplussed in his magic spells and make him concede that you are the superior man in the rules of astronomy and astrology, and for thy glory I will encircle thy brows not with a poet's garland made of bay leaves, but with a coronet of choicest gold. Until the time when we prepare to go to Oxford with our troops, let's go and banquet in our English court."

CHAPTER 5

At Oxford, Ralph the Jester, who was wearing Prince Edward's apparel, and Prince Edward, Warren, and Ermsby talked together. Prince Edward was wearing Ralph's jester outfit, including a coxcomb hat.

Acting as if he were a prince, Ralph the Jester asked, "Where are these rascally knaves, who attend no better on their master?"

"If it pleases your honor, we are all ready to act in an instant on your orders," Prince Edward said.

"Sirrah Ned, I'll have no more post-horse to ride on," the disguised Ralph the Jester said. "I'll have another trick."

"Please tell me, what is that, my lord?" Ermsby asked.

"Indeed, sir, I'll send to the Isle of Ely for four or five dozen geese, and I'll have them tied six and six together with whip-cord," the disguised Ralph the Jester said. "Then upon their backs I will place a fair field-bed with a canopy; and so, when it is my pleasure, I'll flee to whatever place I please. This will be easy."

The Isle of Ely was an area of raised land surrounded by an undrained swamp.

A field-bed is a portable bed used in a military camp.

"Your honor has said well," Warren said, "but shall we go to Brazen-nose College before we pull off our boots?"

"Warren, well proposed," Ermsby said. "We will go to the friar before we party in the town.

"Ralph, see that you keep your countenance — your expression — like that of a prince."

"Why do I have such a company of swaggering knaves to wait upon me, but to keep and defend my countenance — my person — against all my enemies," the disguised Ralph the Jester said. "Haven't you got good swords and shields?"

Friar Bacon and Miles walked near them.

"Hold on," Ermsby said. "Who is coming here?"

"It is some scholar," Warren said, "and we'll ask him where Friar Bacon is."

Friar Bacon said to Miles, "Why, thou unmitigated dunce, shall I never make thee a good scholar? Doesn't all the town cry out and say, 'Friar Bacon's subsizer is the greatest blockhead in all Oxford?'"

A "subsizer" is a "subsidized student." Miles was acting as Friar Bacon's servant in return for free tuition and free room and board.

He continued, "Why, thou cannot speak one word of true Latin."

"I can't, sir?" Miles said. "Yet, what is this other than true Latin? *Ego sum tuus homo*, or 'I am your man.' I promise you, sir, that is as good a Tully's phrase as any is in Oxford."

Tully is Marcus Tullius Cicero, whose use of Latin was and is widely admired.

"Come on, sirrah," Friar Bacon said. "What part of speech is the Latin word '*Ego*'?"

"*Ego*, that is 'I'; indeed, it is *nomen substantivo*."

"*Nomen substantivo*" means "noun substantive."

"How do you prove that?" Friar Bacon asked.

"Why, sir, let it prove itself if it wants to," Miles said. "I can be heard, felt, and understood."

According to *Lily's Grammar of Latin in English* (with modernized spelling), "A noun is the name of a thing that may be seen, felt, heard, or understood." In addition, "A noun substantive is that which stands by himself." Guess which part of a man's body can be seen and felt and stands by himself.

"Oh, you huge dunce!" Friar Bacon said, hitting Miles.

Prince Edward said to his companions, "Come, let's break up this quarrel between these two."

He then asked, "Sirrah, where is Brazen-nose College?"

"Not far from Coppersmith's Hall," Miles answered.

Coppersmith's Hall is a humorous name for an inn. Coppersmiths make things out of copper, which is reddish, and a heavy drinker often makes a red nose in an inn.

"What! Are thou mocking me?" Prince Edward asked.

As a prince, Edward was not accustomed to being treated as an equal by a servant such as Miles.

"Not I, sir," Miles answered, "but what do you want at Brazen-nose?"

"Indeed, we want to speak with Friar Bacon," Ermsby said.

"Whose men are you?" Miles asked, meaning, Whom do you serve?

"Indeed, scholar, here's our master," Ermsby said, pointing to the disguised Ralph the Jester.

"Sirrah, I am the master of these good fellows," the disguised Ralph the Jester said. "Don't thou know me to be a lord by my reparel?"

Although dressed as a prince, Ralph was still a jester. He deliberately used a malapropism here: "reparel" instead of "apparel." The verb "reparel" means "to repair."

"Then here's good prey for the hawk," Miles said, "for here's the master-Fool and a brood of coxcombs. One wise man, I think, would flush all of you out from cover."

"Gog's wounds!" Prince Edward said. "Warren, kill him."

"Gog's wounds!" is an oath meaning "By God's wounds!" "'Swones" means the same thing.

Attempting but failing to take his dagger out of its sheath, Warren said, "Why, Ned, I think the devil is in my sheath; I cannot get out my dagger."

"Nor I mine!" Ermsby said. "'Swones, Ned, I think I am bewitched."

"This is a gang of scoundrels!" Miles said. "The proudest of you all draw your weapon — if he can."

Miles then said to you, the readers of this book, "See how boldly I speak because my master is nearby and is protecting me."

Friar Bacon was protecting him with a spell that prevented anyone from drawing his weapon.

"I strive in vain to draw my sword," Prince Edward said, "but if my sword is fastened and conjured to be stuck fast by magic in my sheath, then, villain, here is my fist."

He hit Miles, who said to Friar Bacon, "Oh, I beg you to conjure his hands, too, so that he may not lift his arms to his head, for he is light-fingered!"

Miles had made a malapropism: He was using "light-fingered" to mean "ready to fight" when it really meant "ready to steal."

"Ned, hit him," the disguised Ralph the Jester said. "I'll back thee up, I swear by my honor."

Friar Bacon asked, "Why does the English prince wrong and injure my man?"

"To whom are you speaking?" Prince Edward asked.

"To thee," Friar Bacon said.

Through magic, Friar Bacon recognized Prince Edward. In addressing him, he dared to use the word "thee" instead of the formal and respectful "you."

"Who are thou?" Prince Edward asked.

Friar Bacon said, "Couldn't you judge when all your swords grew stuck fast that Friar Bacon was not far from here? Edward, King Henry's son and Prince of Wales, thy Fool who is disguised as you cannot conceal thyself.

"I know both Ermsby and Warren, the Earl of Sussex — or else Friar Bacon has but little skill. Thou come in haste from merry Fressingfield, bound by love to the gamekeeper's bonny, pretty lass, to ask for some help from me, the jolly friar. And you have left behind Lacy, Earl of Lincoln, to entreat fair Margaret to allow you to love her. But friends are men, and love can baffle lords. The earl — Lacy — both woos and courts her for himself."

"Ned, this is strange," Warren said. "The friar knows all."

"Apollo, god of prophecy, could not utter more than this," Ermsby said.

"I stand stunned and amazed to hear this jolly friar tell correctly even the very secrets of my thoughts," Prince Edward said to his companions.

He then said, "But, learned Bacon, since thou know the reason why I hastened so fast from Fressingfield, help me, friar, in this important moment, so that I may have the love of lovely Margaret to myself, and as I am the true Prince of Wales, I'll give an endowment and lands to strengthen thy College of Brazen-nose."

"Good friar, help the prince in this," Warren said.

Friar Bacon remained silent.

"Why, servant Ned, won't the friar do it?" the disguised Ralph the Jester said. "If my sword weren't glued to my scabbard by conjuration, I would cut off the friar's head, and make him do it by force."

"In faith, my lord, your manliness and your sword are both alike," Miles said. "They are conjured to be so stuck fast that we shall never see them."

"What, doctor, tongue-tied!" Ermsby said. "Tush, help the prince, and thou shall see how liberal and generous he will prove to be."

"Don't such actions demand greater fits of stupefaction than this one I am experiencing?" Friar Bacon said. "I will, my lord, strain and exert my magic spells because on this day the earl — Lacy — will go to Fressingfield, and before night shuts in the day with dark, he and the gamekeeper's daughter will be betrothed firmly to each other. But come with me; we'll go to my study immediately, and in a magic mirror I will show you what's done this day in merry Fressingfield."

"Thank you, Bacon," Prince Edward said. "I will requite thy pains you take to help me."

"But send your companions, my lord, into the town," Friar Bacon said. "My scholar shall go and bring them to their inn. Meanwhile we'll see the knavery of the earl."

Prince Edward said, "Warren, leave me. And, Ermsby, take the Fool: Let him be your master, and go and have fun until I and Friar Bacon have talked awhile."

"We will, my lord," Warren said.

"Indeed, Ned," the disguised Ralph the Jester said, "I'll lord it out until thou come again. I'll be Prince of Wales over all the people who drink beer from black-leather pots in Oxford."

Warren, Ermsby, Ralph the Jester, and Miles went to the town, while Friar Bacon and Prince Edward went into the friar's study.

CHAPTER 6

Friar Bacon and Prince Edward talked together in Friar Bacon's study. It was now early in the morning.

"Now, merry Edward, welcome to my cell," Friar Bacon said.

Referring to himself in the third person, as he so often did, he continued, "Here Friar Bacon mixes many trifling solutions, and uses this place as his consistory court, wherein the devils plead homage to his words."

A consistory court was a bishop's court used to administer ecclesiastical law.

Friar Bacon showed Prince Edward a magic mirror and said, "Within this magic mirror thou shall see what's done this day in merry Fressingfield between lovely Peggy and Lacy, the Earl of Lincoln."

"Friar, thou gladden me," Prince Edward said.

Using the third person to refer to himself, he continued, "Now Edward shall learn how Lacy is disposed toward his sovereign Lord."

"Stand there and look directly in the mirror," Friar Bacon said.

In the magic mirror, they saw Margaret, who was consulting a magician named Friar Bungay.

Friar Bacon asked, "What does my lord see?"

"I see the gamekeeper's lovely lass appear, as bright-looking as the paramour of Mars, attended only by a jolly friar."

The paramour of Mars, god of war, is Venus, goddess of beauty. Although Venus was married, she had a famous love affair with Mars.

"Sit still, and keep the crystal — the magic mirror — in your sight," Friar Bacon said.

In the magic mirror, Margaret asked, "But tell me, Friar Bungay, is it true that this good-looking, courteous country wooer, who says his father is a farmer not far from here, can be Lord Lacy, Earl of Lincolnshire?"

"Peggy, it is true," Friar Bungay said. "It is Lacy, I swear on my life, or else both my magic and my skill fail. Prince Edward left Lacy behind here so he could procure Prince Edward's love — you — for him. For the man in green, who helped you curdle your cheese, is the son of King Henry the Third — the man in green is the Prince of Wales."

"Be what he will, his luring of me is only for the purpose of satisfying his lust," Margaret said. "But if Lord Lacy were to love poor Margaret, and if he would deign to wed a country lass, Friar, I would be his humble handmaid, and for great wealth I would requite him with courtesy."

The last line is ambiguous. It can mean 1) He would provide me with great financial wealth, and I would repay him with courteous behavior and I would always treat him well, or 2) I would repay him with courteous behavior for the great wealth that is a good and happy marriage — I would always treat him well.

"Why, Margaret, do thou love him?" Friar Bungay asked.

"His appearance, like the pride — Prince Paris — of boasting Troy, might well serve to justify Helen's running away with him: His intelligence is lively and quick in understanding, just like the men Greece produced in its greatest glory."

Paris, a Trojan Prince, had traveled to Sparta and then ran away with Helen, the wife of Menelaus, King of Sparta. Helen became known as Helen of Troy.

Margaret continued, "He is courteous, ah, friar, and full of pleasing smiles! Trust me, I love too much to tell thee more. Suffice it to say that to me he's England's paramour."

To Margaret, Lacy was the best wooer and the greatest darling in all of England.

"Hasn't each man who has viewed thy pleasing face given to you the title of the Fair Maiden of Fressingfield?" Friar Bungay asked.

"Yes, Friar Bungay; and I wish to God that the lovely earl had in *esse* — actuality — that which so many have sought."

"Don't worry," Friar Bungay said. "The friar will not be slow to show his cunning to entangle you two together in love."

Prince Edward said, "I think the friar courts the bonny, pretty wench. Bacon, I think he is a lusty base fellow."

Prince Edward was jealous of Friar Bungay; he was afraid that the friar was pursuing Margaret.

"Now look, my lord," Friar Bacon said.

Lacy entered the scene, disguised as a country fellow as he had previously been when he met Margaret at the fair.

"Gog's wounds, Bacon, here comes Lacy!" Prince Edward said.

"Sit still, my lord, and closely observe the comedy," Friar Bacon said.

A comedy is a story with a happy ending.

"Here's Lacy coming, Margaret," Friar Bungay said. "Step aside for awhile and don't be seen."

He and Margaret hid themselves.

Talking to himself, Earl Lacy of Lincoln said, "Daphne, the damsel who caught Phoebus Apollo fast in love, and locked him in the brightness of her looks, was not as beauteous in Apollo's eyes as is fair Margaret to the Earl of Lincoln.

"Recant these words of yours, Lacy — thou are on an errand of trust. Edward, thy sovereign's son, has chosen thee, a friend who knows his secrets, a friend who is his confidant, to court her for himself, and dare thou wrong thy prince with treachery?

"Lacy, Love makes no exception for a friend, nor treats a man as a prince but only as a man. Love treats everyone equally. Love doesn't care if you are wooing in behalf of a friend, or if you are a prince.

"Honor bids thee to restrain Prince Edward in his lust: His wooing is not for the purpose of wedding the girl, but instead to entrap and deceive the lass. Lacy, thou love her, so then don't tolerate such intended abuse of her, but instead wed her, and endure thy prince's disapproval, for it is better to die than to see her live as a disgraced woman."

"Come, friar, I will shake him out of his depression," Margaret said. "I will cheer him up."

She came out from hiding and said to Lacy, "How are you, sir? A penny for your thoughts. You're early up, and I pray to God it be the near."

A proverb stated, "Early up and never the nearer." It meant that someone had gotten up early to accomplish something but had failed to make progress on that thing. Margaret was hoping that Lacy, who had gotten up early, was getting near to accomplishing her hope of his marrying her.

Margaret then asked, "Why have you come from Beccles in the morning so soon?"

"Thus wakeful are such men as live in love, whose eyes endure broken slumbers instead of uninterrupted sleep," Lacy said. "I tell thee, Peggy, since Harleston Fair my mind has felt a multitude of passionate emotions."

"A faithful man, who court it for your friend," Margaret said. "Do you still woo for the courtier all in green? I marvel that he woos not for himself. He should do his own wooing."

"Peggy, I pleaded at first to get your grace for him — I wanted to get you to like him," Lacy said. "But when my eyes surveyed your beauteous looks, Love, like a mischievous fellow, immediately dived into my heart, and there he enshrined the idea — the image — of yourself."

The god of love is Cupid, who is portrayed as a mischievous fellow.

Lacy continued, "Pity me, although I am a farmer's son, and measure me not by my wealth, but by my love."

By "wealth," Lacy meant a farmer's wealth, not an earl's wealth. He was still pretending to be the son of a farmer.

"You are very hasty," Margaret said, "for to garden well, seeds must have time to sprout before they fully emerge. Love ought to creep as does the sundial's shadow, for too-soon ripe is too-too soon rotten."

Friar Bungay came out of hiding and said, *"Deus hic!"*

"Deus hic" means "God is in this place!" In other words, this match is something that God will surely approve of.

He continued, "Make room for a merry friar! What! Do I see the youth of Beccles with the gamekeeper's lass? It is well; but tell me, have you heard any news?"

"No, friar," Margaret replied. "What news?"

"Haven't you heard how the pursuivants — the royal messengers — ride posthaste with proclamations through each country-town?"

"Why, gentle friar?" Lacy said. "Tell us the news."

"Do thou live in Beccles, and haven't heard the news?" Friar Bungay said. "Lacy, the Earl of Lincoln, has recently fled from the court at Windsor Castle, disguised like a countryman, and he lurks about the country here unknown.

"Henry the Third suspects him of some treachery, and therefore proclaims on every road that whoever can capture the Earl of Lincoln shall have, paid in the Exchequer — the royal treasury — twenty thousand crowns."

"The Earl of Lincoln!" Lacy said. "Friar, thou are mad. It was some other person; thou are mistaken about the man. The Earl of Lincoln! Why, it cannot be."

"Yes, very well, my lord, for you are he," Margaret said. "The gamekeeper's daughter has taken you prisoner. Lord Lacy, yield. I'll be your jailer for this occasion."

"Look at how familiar they are with each other, Bacon!" Prince Edward said.

"Sit still, and observe closely the sequel of their loves," Friar Bacon said. "See what happens next."

"Then I am doubly a prisoner to thyself. Peggy, I yield myself to you. I am your legal prisoner and your love prisoner. But is this news in jest?"

Yes, it was.

"In jest with you, but earnest to me," Margaret said, "because these wrongs press down on me at the heart. Ah, how these earls and noblemen of birth flatter and deceive to forge evil for poor women!"

"Believe me, lass," Lacy said. "I am the Earl of Lincoln. I do not deny that; however, attired thus in rags, I lived disguised to win fair Peggy's love."

"What love is there where love does not lead to a wedding?" Margaret said, referring to Lacy's attempt to win her love for Prince Edward.

Lacy replied, "I intend, beautiful girl, to make thee Lacy's wife."

"I little think that earls will stoop so low," Margaret said. "They will not marry so far beneath their social class."

"Tell me: Shall I make thee a countess before I sleep?" Lacy said. "I am willing to marry thee this very day."

The wife of an earl is a countess.

"A handmaid to the earl, if he so wishes: A wife in name, but a servant in obedience," Margaret said.

To the Elizabethans, a good wife is an obedient wife. Margaret was saying that as his wife, she would be as obedient as a servant. But in addition, she was expressing a fear that even if she were his wife, he might treat her as merely a lower-class servant.

"The Lincoln Countess, for it shall be so," Lacy said.

He was saying that he would treat her as a countess, not as a servant.

He continued, "I'll pledge myself to the bonds of marriage, and seal my pledge with a kiss."

This was a formal pledge of engagement that shall be followed by a wedding.

"Gog's wounds, Bacon, they kiss!" Prince Edward said. "I'll stab them!"

He drew his dagger and moved toward the magic mirror.

"Oh, restrain your hands, my lord," Friar Bacon said. "It is the mirror you are about to attack!"

"My rage at seeing the traitors match so well made me think that the shadows in the mirror are real substances," Prince Edward said.

"It would take a long dagger, my lord, to reach from Oxford here to Fressingfield there," Friar Bacon said, "but sit still and see more."

"Well, Lord of Lincoln, if your loves are united, and if your words and thoughts both agree, to avoid any future discords, I'll quickly make the marriage official," Friar Bungay said. "I'll take my portace — my portable Catholic book of prayers — out and wed you here. Then you can go to bed and consummate your desires."

"Friar, this is good," Lacy said.

He then asked, "Peggy, how do you like this? Does it please you?"

"What pleases my lord pleases me," Margaret said.

"Then join hands, and I will go to the relevant passage — the words of the wedding ceremony — in my book," Friar Bungay said.

"What does my lord see now?" Friar Bacon asked.

"Bacon, I see the lovers hand in hand, and I see the friar ready with his portace there to wed them both," Prince Edward said. "So then I am quite ruined. Bacon, help me now, if ever thy magic served someone. Help me, Bacon; stop the marriage now, if devils or necromancy may suffice to do so, and I will give thee forty thousand crowns."

"Fear not, my lord, I'll stop the jolly friar from mumbling — speaking — his prayers this day," Friar Bacon said.

He cast a spell that made Friar Bungay unable to say anything other than nonsense syllables.

Friar Bungay tried to speak, but he could say only, "Hud, hud."

"Why don't you speak, Bungay?" Lacy asked. "Friar, read out loud the wedding ceremony in thy book."

"Why is it that thou look, friar, like a man distraught?" Margaret said. "Are you bereft of thy senses, Bungay? Show by signs, if thou are unable to speak, what illness has seized thee."

"He's dumb — unable to talk — indeed," Lacy said. "Friar Bacon has with his devils enchanted him, or else some strange disease or apoplexy has possessed his lungs: But, Peggy, what he cannot do with his book because of his muteness, we'll do between us and unite ourselves in our hearts."

In this culture, a man and a woman could make private vows of intent to wed that were legally binding.

"Or else let me die, my lord, an unbeliever," Margaret said.

This culture believed that unbelievers went to Hell.

"Why does Friar Bungay stand so dumbfounded?" Prince Edward asked.

"I have struck him dumb, my lord," Friar Bacon replied, "and if it pleases your honor, I'll fetch this Bungay immediately from Fressingfield, and he shall dine with us in Oxford here."

"Bacon, if thou do that, thou will please me," Prince Edward said.

"Out of courtesy, because we ought to do it, Margaret, let us lead the friar to thy father's lodge, to comfort him with broths to bring him out of this luckless trance," Lacy said.

"If we did not help him, my lord, we would be extremely unkind to leave this friar so in his distress," Margaret said.

A devil arrived and carried away Bungay on his back.

"Oh, help, my lord!" Margaret said. "A devil, a devil, my lord! Look how he carries Bungay on his back! Let's go away from here, for Bacon's spirits are abroad."

"Bacon, I laugh to see the jolly friar mounted upon the devil and to see how the earl flees with his bonny, pretty lass out of fear," Prince Edward said. "As soon as Bungay is at Brazen-nose, and I have chatted with the merry friar, I will quickly go to Fressingfield, and repay these wrongs on Lacy before much time passes."

"So be it, my lord," Friar Bacon said, "but let us go to our dinner for before we have had time to eat much, we shall have Bungay brought to Brazen-nose."

CHAPTER 7

— Scene 7 —

Burden, Mason, and Clement talked together in the Regent House at Oxford. These Oxford doctors and administrators were preparing for the visit of King Henry III and his visitors and entourage.

"Now that we are gathered in the Regent House, it befits us to talk about the king's soon-to-occur visit," Mason said, "for in their revels he has decided to make a royal journey to visit the town of Oxford. He is accompanied by all the western kings — those who lie along the Baltic Sea by east, and north by the region of frosty Germany. The dignitaries with him include the Almain monarch, and the Duke of Saxony, the King of Castile, and lovely Eleanor, the King of Castile's daughter."

The Almain monarch is the Emperor of Germany.

"We must make detailed plans to stage dignified tragedies and exotic, amusing masques and pageants, such as the proud Roman actor Roscius proudly presented before the Roman emperors, to welcome all the western potentates," Burden said.

"But there is more," Clement said. "The king by letters has given us notice that Frederick, the Emperor of Germany, has brought with him a German of great reputation. His name is Don Jacques Vandermast, and he is skilled in magic and those secret arts."

"Then we all must ask Friar Bacon to agree to take on this task of undertaking to compete in skill with the German," Mason said. "No one else in Oxford can match and dispute with learned Vandermast."

"Bacon, if he will compete against the German Vandermast, will teach him what an English friar can do," Burden said. "The devil, I think, does not dare to dispute with Bacon."

"Indeed, Mas Doctor," Clement said, "he 'pleasured' you, in that he brought your hostess with her spit, from Henley, hastening her to Brazen-nose."

"Mas" meant "Master" — a title of respect.

"A vengeance on the friar for his deeds!" Burden said. "But leaving that aside, let's hurry immediately to Bacon to see if he will take this task in hand."

They heard lots of noise and shouting.

"Wait, what clamor is this?" Clement said. "The town is up in an uproar. What hurly-burly and commotion is this I hear?"

A constable entered with Ralph the Jester, Warren, and Ermsby, all three still dressed as previously. Miles accompanied them. Ralph the Jester was still disguised as Prince Edward.

The constable said, "Masters, even if you were never so good, you shall go before the doctors to answer for your misdemeanor."

"What's the matter, fellow?" Burden asked.

"Indeed, sir, here's a company of rogues, who, drinking in the tavern, have made a great brawl and almost killed the tavern keeper," the constable replied.

"*Salve*, Doctor Burden!" Miles said.

"*Salve*" is a Latin greeting used as we use "Hello."

He began to speak in bad poetry:

"This lubberly lurden

"Ill-shaped and ill-faced,

["Misshapen and ugly,]

"Disdained and disgraced,

"What he tells unto *vobis*,

["What he tells to all of you,]

"*Mentitur de nobis*."

[About us is false."]

Remarkably, Miles was a fan of John Skelton, King Henry VIII of England's Poet Laureate. Miles' verse was Skeltonic in form. What is remarkable about this is that neither King Henry VIII nor John Skelton would be born until centuries had passed.

"Who is the master and chief of this crew?" Burden asked.

Miles said:

"*Ecce asinum mundi*,

["Behold the ass of the world,]

"*Fugura [should be 'Figura'] rotundi*,

["With a figure as round as the world,]

"Neat, sheat, and fine,

["Undiluted, trim and neat, and fine,]

"As brisk as a cup of wine."

"Who are you?" Burden asked.

"I am, father doctor, as a man would say, the bell-wether of this company," Ralph the Jester replied.

He meant that he was the leader of this company. A wether is a male sheep, and the bell-wether is the male leader of the other sheep and wears a bell.

He continued, "These are my lords, and I am the Prince of Wales."

"Are you Edward, the king's son?" Clement asked.

"Sirrah Miles, bring here the tavern-keeper who drew the wine from the barrel, and, I promise you, when they see how soundly I have broken his head, they'll say it was done by no less man than a prince."

"I cannot believe that this is the Prince of Wales," Mason said.

"And why so, sir?" Warren asked.

"Because they say the prince is a brave and a wise gentleman," Mason answered.

"Why, and do thou say, doctor, that he is not so?" Warren replied. "Do thou dare detract from and derogate him, who is so lovely and so finely dressed a youth?"

"His face, shining with many a sugary-sweet smile, reveals that he is bred of princely race," Ermsby said.

Miles said:

"And yet, master doctor,

"To speak like a proctor,"

A proctor is in charge of discipline at a British university.

Miles continued:

"And tell unto you

"What is veriment [the truth] and true;

"To put an end to this quarrel,

"Look but on his apparel;

"Then mark [pay attention to] but my talis [tale],

"He is great Prince of Walis [Wales],

"The chief of our *gregis* [flock],

"And *filius regis* [son of the king]:

"Then 'ware [be wary; be careful] what is done,

"For he is Henry's white [dear] son."

Ralph the Jester said, "Doctors, whose foolish nightcaps" — literally, he was referring to the soft caps worn by academic doctors; figuratively, he was referring to the doctors' heads — "are not capable of understanding my ingenious intellectual dignity, know that I am Edward Plantagenet, whom if you displease, will make a ship that shall hold all your colleges, and so carry away the ninniversity" — a ninniversity is a university filled with ninnies — "with a fair wind to the Bankside in Southwark."

In other words, he was going to load the academic doctors on a ship of fools and sail them to the south bank of the Thames River, where were located the theaters and many, many prostitutes.

He then asked, "What do thou say, Ned Warren? Shall I not do it?"

"Yes, my good lord," Warren said, "and, if it please your lordship, I will gather up all your old pantofles — cork-soled shoes — and with the cork make you a pinnace — a small boat — weighing five-hundred tons" — a vast exaggeration — "that shall serve the purpose marvelously well, my lord."

"And I, my lord, will have military pioneers undermine the town, so that the very gardens and orchards are carried away for your summer-walks," Ermsby said.

Pioneers were army laborers who did such things as dig tunnels — called mines — under the walls of fortifications. They would plant explosives in the mines and blow up the wall.

Miles said:

"And I, with *scientia* [science],

"And great *diligentia* [diligence],

"Will conjure and charm,

"To keep you from harm;

"That [So that] *utrum horum mavis* [whichever of these you prefer],

"Your very great *navis* [ship],

"Like Bartlett's [actually Barclay's; in 1509, Alexander Barclay's book *The Ship of Fools* was published] ship,

"From Oxford do skip

"With colleges and schools,

"Full-loaden [Fully loaded] with fools.

"*Quid dicis ad hoc,*

["What do you say to that,]

"Worshipful *Domine* [Lord] Dawcock?"

A dawcock is a male jackdaw; here it means "fool" because fools are often said to be bird-brained as well as hare-brained.

"Why, hare-brained courtiers, are you drunk or mad? Is that why you taunt us with such scurrility?" Clement said. "Do you deem us men of base and light esteem and so you bring us such a fop — such a buffoon — and claim he is Henry the Third's son?

"Call out the beadles and convey them from here immediately to Bocardo — Oxford's prison. Let these roisters — boisterous revelers — lie shut up in prison and clapped in fetters until their wits are tame and they have calmed down."

"Why, shall we go to prison, my lord?" Ermsby asked.

"What do you say, Miles, shall I honor the prison with my presence?" Ralph the Jester asked.

Miles replied:

"No, no; out with your blades [draw your swords],

"And hamper [beat] these jades [broken-down horses];

"Have a flurt and a crash,

["Make an attack and crash bodies together,]

"Now play revel-dash,

["Now fight joyfully,]

"And teach these sacerdos"

Sacerdos is Latin for "a priest," but Miles was using it to mean "priests."

He continued:

"That the Bocardos [university jail cells],

"Like peasants and elves,

"Are meet [suitable] for themselves."

"To the prison with them, constable," Mason said.

"Well, doctors," Warren said, "seeing I have entertained myself with laughing at these mad and merry jokers, know that Prince Edward is at Brazen-nose, and this man, who is attired like the Prince of Wales, is Ralph, King Henry's especially loved Fool; I am the Earl of Sussex, and this man is Ermsby, who is one of the king's chamberlains — he has access to the king's personal rooms. All of us, while the prince stays with Friar Bacon, have partied in Oxford as you see."

"My lord, pardon us, we didn't know who you were," Mason said. "But the king's courtiers may engage in greater escapades than these. Will it please your honor to dine with me today?"

"I will, Master Doctor, and I will recompense the vintner for his hurt," Warren said. "But I must request you to imagine him — Ralph the Jester — all the rest of this morning as the Prince of Wales. Pretend that he is Prince Edward."

"I will, sir," Mason said.

"And on that condition I will lead the way," Ralph the Jester said, "only I will have Miles go before me, because I have heard Henry say that wisdom must go before majesty."

CHAPTER 8

— Scene 8 —

At Fressingfield, Prince Edward, with his dagger in his hand, faced Lacy and Margaret.

"Lacy, thou cannot conceal thy traitorous thoughts, nor hide, as did Cassius, all thy treachery," Prince Edward said, "for Edward has an eye that sees as far as Lynceus from the shores of Graecia."

Cassius, along with Brutus and other conspirators, assassinated Julies Caesar. To do that successfully, Cassius and the others had to keep the plot secret.

Lynceus was an Argonaut whose eyesight was so keen that he could see objects that had been buried in the ground. He could also see people who were vast distances away.

"Didn't I sit in Oxford by Friar Bacon and see thee court the maiden of Fressingfield, sealing thy flattering fancies — your love — with a kiss?" Prince Edward said. "Didn't proud Bungay draw his portace forth, and joining your hand in her hand would have married you two if Friar Bacon had not struck him dumb and mounted him upon a spirit's back, so that we might chat at Oxford with Friar Bungay? Traitor, what do you answer! Isn't all this true?"

"It is all true, my lord; and thus I make reply," Lacy said. "At Harleston Fair, I was courting on behalf of your grace, when my eye surveyed her exquisite shape and drew the beauteous glory of her looks to dive into the center of my heart. Love taught me that your honor did but jest and was not serious about loving her and that princes were in love only as men. Love made me believe that the lovely maiden of Fressingfield was fitter to be Lacy's wedded wife than to be a concubine to the Prince of Wales."

"Injurious Lacy, did I love thee more than Alexander loved his Hephaestion?"

Alexander the Great and Hephaestion, one of his generals, were best friends since childhood. When Hephaestion died, Alexander held an extravagant funeral for him.

Prince Edward continued, "Did I reveal the passions of my love, and lock them in the closet of thy thoughts? Were thou to Edward second to himself, sole friend, and confidant of his secret loves? And could a glance of beauty that will fade break the linked chains of such private friends?

"Base coward, false, and too effeminate to be a partner with a prince in thoughts! Like a woman, you have let your emotions rule you. From Oxford I have ridden since I dined to repay a traitor before I, Edward, sleep."

"It was I, my lord, not Lacy, who stepped awry," Margaret said. "Often he frequently sued and courted for yourself, and always he wooed for the courtier dressed all in green, but I, whom love made but over-fond and over-foolish, sent Lacy looks that showed him I loved him. I pleaded my own case to him with looks that showed I was in love with him.

"I fed my eye with gazing on his face, and I continually bewitched my beloved Lacy with my looks. My heart pleaded with sighs, my eyes pleaded with tears, my face held pity and contentment at the same time, and I could not express anything more by nonverbal signs, other than that I loved Lord Lacy with all my heart. So then, worthy Edward, measure with thy mind whether women's favors will not force men to fall in love with her and whether beauty and arrows of piercing love are not offered to bury thoughts of friends. A woman's loving attention can cause a man to forget his friends."

"I tell thee, Peggy," Prince Edward said. "I will have thy loves; Edward or none shall conquer Margaret. In frigates bottomed with rich acacia-wood planks, topped with the lofty firs of Lebanon, hulled and encased with polished ivory, and over-laid with gold leaf of Persian wealth, like Thetis thou shall frolic on the waves, and draw the dolphins to thy lovely eyes, to dance lively leaping, lavolta dances in the purple streams of water."

In mythology, Thetis is a sea-nymph who is the mother of Achilles, the greatest warrior of the Trojan War.

Prince Edward continued, "Sirens, with harps and silver psalteries — stringed instruments — shall serve you by playing music at thy frigate's prow and entertaining fair Margaret with their songs."

Sirens sang beautiful songs to entice sailors to sail too close to shore and wreck their ships on the rocks.

Prince Edward continued, "England and England's wealth shall wait on thee; Britain shall figuratively bend her knee to her prince's love and do due homage to thine excellence, if thou will just be Edward's Margaret."

"Give me pardon, my lord," Margaret said. "If Jove's great royalty sent me such presents as he sent to Danae, that still could not make me leave Lord Lacy or his love."

Jupiter, king of the gods, became a shower of gold in order to visit Danae.

"If Phoebus Apollo, attired in Latona's fabrics, should come courting from the beauty of his lodge, that still could not make me leave Lord Lacy or his love."

Latona, whose Greek name is Leto, is the mother of Apollo and Diana, whose Greek name is Artemis.

"Neither the dulcet tunes of frolic Mercury, inventor of the musical instruments called the lyre and the shepherd's pipe, nor all the wealth that Heaven's treasury can provide, would make me leave Lord Lacy or his love."

"I have learned at Oxford, then, this aphorism of schools — *Abata causa, tollitur effectus*," Prince Edward said.

The Latin means, "The cause being removed, the effect will fail." In other words: Kill Lacy, and Margaret will cease to love him. Prince Edward was hoping that if Margaret ceased to love Lacy, then she would love him.

He continued, "Lacy is the cause that Margaret cannot love nor fix her liking on the English prince. Take him away, and then the effect will fail."

He then said to Lacy, "Villain, prepare thyself; for I will bathe my dagger in the bosom of an earl."

"Rather than that I live, and lose fair Margaret's love, Prince Edward, don't stop at only saying the fatal judgment you have made against me, but instead stab your dagger home in my heart," Lacy said. "End both my love and my life."

"Brave Prince of Wales, honored for royal deeds," Margaret said, "it would be a sin to stain fair Venus' courts with blood. Love's conquests end, my lord, in courtesy. Spare Lacy, gentle Edward; let me die because that way both you and he will cease to love me."

She meant that once they ceased to love her, Prince Edward and Lacy could again be friends.

"Lacy shall die as a traitor to his lord," Prince Edward said.

"I have deserved it, Edward," Lacy said. "Carry out the punishment well."

"What does the prince hope to gain by Lacy's death?" Margaret asked.

"To end the love between him and Margaret," Prince Edward answered.

Margaret said, "Why, does King Henry's son think that Margaret's love hangs in the uncertain balance of proud time? Do you think that she will forget Lacy with time? Do you think that death shall make a discord of Lacy's and my thoughts about each other! No, slay the earl, and, before the morning sun shall proudly rise three times over the lofty east, Margaret will meet her Lacy in the Heavens."

In other words, within three days after Lacy dies she will commit suicide or die of heartbreak.

"If anything should happen to lovely Margaret that wrongs or wrings her honor away from happiness, then neither Europe's rich wealth nor England's monarchy would tempt Lacy to stretch out his life and outlive her," Lacy said. "So then, Edward, shorten my life, and end her love for me."

"Get rid of me by killing me, and keep a friend worth many loves," Margaret said.

"Nay, Edward, keep a love worth many friends," Lacy said.

"And if thy disposition is such as Fame has proclaimed it to be, then, princely Edward, let us both bear the fatal resolution of thy rage," Margaret said. "Banish love, and embrace revenge: Kill both Lacy and me, and in one tomb unite both our carcasses, whose hearts were linked in one perfect love."

Prince Edward thought, *Edward, are thou that famous Prince of Wales, who at Damascus beat the Saracens, and brought home triumph on thy lance's point? And shall thy feathers in thy helmet be pulled down by Venus? Is it princely to dissever lovers' leagues, to separate such friends as exult in their loves? Stop this, Ned, and instead make a virtue of this fault, and assist Peg and Lacy in their loves: So in subduing fancy's passion, conquering thyself, thou get the richest spoil.*

Prince Edward conquered his strong emotions as if they were the enemy; in doing so, he reaped great spoils — the knowledge that he was doing the right thing.

Prince Edward then said, "Lacy, rise up.

"Fair Peggy, here's my hand." — They shook hands. — "The Prince of Wales has conquered all his thoughts, and all his love for you he yields to the earl.

"Lacy, enjoy the maiden of Fressingfield; make her thy Countess of Lincoln at the church, and Ned, as he is true Plantagenet, will give her to thee unconditionally for thy wife."

"Humbly I take her from my sovereign," Lacy said. "Your giving Margaret to me is just as if you, Edward, were giving me England's throne and were enriching me with the crown of Albion."

Albion is the ancient name for Britain.

"And does the English prince say the truth?" Margaret asked. "Will he graciously cease his former love of me, and yield his claim to a country maiden to Lord Lacy?"

"I will, fair Peggy, as I am a true lord," Prince Edward said.

Margaret said, "Then, lordly sir, whose conquest is as great in conquering love, as Caesar's victories, Margaret, as mild and humble in her thoughts as was Aspasia to Cyrus himself, yields thanks, and, after Lord Lacy, enshrines Edward as the next closest in her heart."

Persian Emperor Cyrus the Younger loved his favorite concubine, Aspasia, whom he called "The Wise." He also called her a "free and unperverted woman" the first time he met her.

"Gramercy, Peggy," Prince Edward said.

"Gramercy" means "great thanks."

He continued, "Now that your vows are exchanged with each other, and now that your loves are not to be withdrawn, we are, Lacy, friends once again. Come, we will ride to Oxford; for this day the king is there, and he brings for Edward Eleanor from Castile.

"Peggy, I must go see and view my wife. I pray God I like her as I loved thee.

"Besides, Lord Lincoln, we shall witness a competition between Friar Bacon and learned Vandermast.

"Peggy, we'll leave you for a week or two."

"As it pleases Lord Lacy," Margaret said, "do so, but love's foolish looks think that footsteps are miles and that minutes are hours. Each footstep you are away from me seems to be a mile, and each second you are away from me seems to be an hour."

"I'll hasten, Peggy, to make a quick return," Lacy said.

He then said to Prince Edward, "But may it please your honor to go to the lodge. We shall have butter, cheese, and venison. And yesterday I brought for Margaret a robust bottle of pure claret-wine. Thus we can feast and entertain your grace."

"It is hospitality, Lord Lacy, for an emperor, if he respect the person and the place," Prince Edward said.

He meant that even though he would dine in a humble gamekeeper's lodge, it would be as if he were dining as an emperor would because he loved the hosts and the place: It is the company that makes the meal.

He added, "Come, let us go in; for I will all this night ride posthaste until I come to Friar Bacon's cell."

CHAPTER 9

King Henry III of England, the Emperor of Germany, the King of Castile, Eleanor (the King of Castile's daughter), Jacques Vandermast the German magician, and Friar Bungay met together.

"Trust me, Plantagenet, the Oxford schools are splendidly located near the riverside," the Emperor of Germany said.

Oxford is located at the junction of the Thames River and the Cherwell River.

The Emperor continued, "The mountains are full of fat and brown-colored deer, the nourishing pastures are laden with cattle and flocks, the town is gorgeous with high-built colleges, and the scholars are seemly in their grave attire and learned in seeking the principles of the liberal arts.

"What is thy opinion, Jacques Vandermast?"

"That lordly are the buildings of the town, spacious the open places and full of pleasant walks — but as for the doctors, how that they be learned, it may be meanly, for anything I can hear," Vandermast replied.

"I tell thee, German, Hapsburg holds none such, none who are read as deeply as the scholars Oxford contains," Friar Bungay said. "There are within our academic state men who may lecture in Germany to all the doctors of your schools."

"Stand up to him, Bungay," King Henry III said. "Charm and defeat this Vandermast with your magic spells, and I will treat thee as a royal king should."

"In what areas of knowledge and art do thou dare dispute — formally debate — with me?" Vandermast asked Friar Bungay.

"In those areas that a scholar and a friar can debate," Friar Bungay replied.

Vandermast said, "Here in front of rich Europe's worthiest men, put forth the difficult question of this debate to Vandermast."

"Let it be this question: Which spirits — those of pyromancy or those of geomancy — are the most predominant in magic?" Friar Bungay said.

Spirits of pyromancy are spirits of fire; spirits of geomancy are spirits of earth.

According to this culture, reality is made of four elements: fire, earth, water, and air. Certain spirits are associated with each of the four elements.

"I say, of pyromancy," Vandermast said.

"And I, of geomancy," Friar Bungay said.

"The cabalists — men skilled in magic — who write of magic spells, such as Hermes, Melchie, and Pythagoras, affirm that, among the quadruplicity of elemental essence, *terra* is only thought to be a *punctum* squared to the rest," Vandermast said.

Hermes Trismegistus was an alchemist, and Malchus Porphyry (called here "Melchie") was a Neoplatonist. Pythagoras was the famous mathematician and philosopher.

The "quadruplicity of elemental essence" are the four elements. "*Terra*" is earth. "A *punctum* squared to the rest" means a point or atom of little importance compared to (or measured by) the rest of the elements.

Vandermast was denigrating earth as an element; according to the authorities he cited, it is the least important of the four elements.

He continued, "They also say that the compass — circumference — of ascending elements exceed in bigness as they do in height; they judge that the concave circle of the Sun holds the rest in his circumference. If, then, as Hermes says, the fire is the greatest, purest, and preeminent sphere to give shape to spirits, then these demons that frequent that place — the sphere of fire — must be in every way superior to the rest."

According to this culture, the four elements have their own spheres. Earth is at the center. Next come the sphere of water, the sphere of air, and the sphere of fire. According to Vandermast, the higher the sphere, the more powerful its element is. Fire is the highest of the four spheres, and so fire is the most powerful element, and therefore spirits of fire are the most powerful spirits.

In Ptolemaic astronomy, the sphere of fire is between the sphere of air and the sphere of the Moon. Then come the spheres of Mercury, Venus, and the Sun.

Vandermast had said that "the concave circle of the Sun holds the rest in his circumference." If he meant that the sphere of the Sun was larger than the spheres of fire, air, water, and earth, then he was correct, but the sphere of the Sun is not the Ptolemaic sphere of fire.

People of the Middle Ages and the Renaissance debated whether the sphere of fire existed. In Christopher Marlowe's *Doctor Faustus*, Mephistophilis tells Faust that the sphere of fire does not exist. In Dante's *Paradise*, Dante the Pilgrim and Beatrice pass through the sphere of fire as they rise from the Forest of Eden at the top of the Mountain of Purgatory to the Moon.

Friar Bungay replied, "I will not talk about elemental shapes — the spheres of the elements.

"Nor will I talk about the concave latitudes — the spherical volumes.

"Nor will I talk about their essence or their quality — their characteristics.

"Those topics are irrelevant to the question at hand.

"But I will talk about the spirits that pyromancy summons, and I will talk about the vigor and power of the geomantic fiends. I tell thee, German, magic haunts the grounds, and those strange necromantic spells that work such shows and sights and wondering in the world are acted by those geomantic spirits that Hermes called *terrae filii* — sons of the earth. The fiery spirits are only transparent shadows that lightly pass as heralds to bear news. But earthly fiends, closed in the lowest deep, split mountains, if they are only commanded to do so. The spirits of the earth are greater and more substantial in their power than are the spirits of fire."

Vandermast replied, "Rather these earthly geomantic spirits are dull and like the place where they remain because when proud Lucifer fell from the Heavens after rebelling against god, the spirits and angels that did sin with him, retained their local essence — their defining characteristics — just as they retained their faults, all subjected under Luna's continent. They that offended the least hung in the fire, and they that offended second least rested within the air. But Lucifer and his proud-hearted fiends were thrown into the center of the Earth because they had less understanding than the rest, and because they had greater sin and lesser grace. Therefore, such dull and earthly spirits serve jugglers, witches, and vile sorcerers. In contrast, the pyromantic genii are mighty, swift, and of far-reaching power."

When Lucifer rebelled against God, he was thrown down from Heaven to the Earth. Dante's *Divine Comedy* states that Lucifer fell with such force that he ended up at the exact center of the Earth. In falling, he created a passage to the center of the Earth that became Hell, which according to Dante has nine circles. Lucifer is in the ninth, and lowest, circle. The land that Lucifer displaced when he fell to the center of the Earth became the Mountain of Purgatory.

According to Vandermast, the angels that fell with Lucifer are all under the sphere of Luna the Moon, but they occupy different spheres according to the severity of their sin. In Dante, all of the rebelling angels are in the Inferno.

Vandermast continued, "But for the sake of argument, let us grant that geomancy has the most force. Bungay, to please these mighty potentates who are here before us, prove by some instance what thy magical art can do."

"I will," Bungay replied.

"Now, English Harry, here begins the game," King Henry III said to himself. "We shall see an entertaining competition between these learned men."

"What will thou do?" Vandermast asked.

"I will show thee the tree, leaved with refined gold, on which the fear-causing dragon held his seat. This dragon guarded the garden called Hesperides, but was subdued and conquered by conquering Hercules."

In the garden of the Hesperides, a dragon with a hundred heads guarded a tree with the golden apples, and Heracles fought and defeated the dragon and took some of the golden apples as one of his famous labors. "Hesperides" is the name of the goddesses of the garden and of the garden itself.

Friar Bungay conjured, and the tree appeared with the dragon shooting fire.

"Well done," Vandermast said, but he intended to do better.

"What do you say, royal lordings, to my friar?" King Henry III asked. "Hasn't he done a fine example of his cunning skill?"

"Each and every scholar of the necromantic spells can do as much as Bungay has performed!" Vandermast said. "But since Alcmena's bastard razed this tree, I will raise him up as when he lived, and cause him to pull down the dragon from his seat, and tear the branches to pieces from the root — the trunk — of the tree."

Hercules' mother was Alcmena, but his father was Jupiter rather than Alcmena's mortal husband, and so Hercules was a bastard. Hercules actually did not raze — destroy — the tree with the golden apples; he merely took some of the tree's golden apples.

"Hercules! *Prodi! Prodi*, Hercules!"

"*Prodi!*" is Latin for "Come forth!"

A spirit impersonating Hercules appeared in his lion's skin.

"*Quis me vult?*" the spirit impersonating Hercules asked.

["Who wants me?" the spirit impersonating Hercules asked.]

"Jove's bastard son, thou Libyan Hercules, pull the sprigs off the Hesperian tree, as once thou did to win the golden fruit."

Vandermast called Hercules "Libyan" because while in Libya on his way to the land of the Hesperides to obtain the golden apples, Heracles met Antaeus, who challenged him to a wrestling match — the loser of the wrestling match would forfeit his life. Antaeus did this to collect the skulls of travelers so that when he had enough, he could build a temple out of them to Poseidon, his father. The mother of Antaeus was Gaia, the goddess of the Earth. As long as Antaeus touched Gaia, he regained his strength. After throwing Antaeus to the earth a few times, Heracles discovered this secret, and he defeated Antaeus by strangling him while holding him up in the air so that Antaeus' feet did not touch the Earth.

"*Fiat,*" the spirit impersonating Hercules replied.

["Let it be done," the spirit impersonating Hercules replied.]

He began to break the branches.

"Now, Bungay, if thou can by magic dissuade the fiend that appears like great Hercules from pulling down the branches of the tree, then thou are worthy to be accounted a learned man."

"I cannot," Friar Bungay said.

"Cease, Hercules, until I give thee the order to start again," Vandermast said.

He then said, "Mighty commander of this English isle, Henry, come from the brave Plantagenets, Bungay is learned enough to be a friar, but to find someone to compare with Jacques Vandermast, Oxford and Cambridge must go and search through all their cells to find a man to match him in his art.

"I have baffled the Paduans, and I have baffled them of Siena, Florence, and Bologna, Rheims, Louvain, and fair Rotterdam, Frankfort, Utrecht, and Orleans. And now Henry must, if he will treat me right, crown me with a wreath of laurel, as they all have done."

Friar Bacon entered the scene.

"All hail to this royal company, who sit to hear and see this strange dispute!" he said. "Bungay, why do thou stand as a man stunned! Has the German performed more than thou?"

"Who are thou who asks these questions?" Vandermast asked.

"Men call me Bacon."

"Thou look lordly, as if thou were learned," Vandermast said. "Thy countenance is as if science occupied a position of authority between the circled arches of thy brows."

"Now, monarchs, the German has found his match," King Henry III said.

"Bestir thee, Jacques, and don't be defeated, lest thou lose what previously thou did gain," the Emperor of Germany said.

"Bacon, will thou dispute?" Vandermast asked.

"No, not unless I dispute with a man who is more learned than Vandermast," Bacon said, "but still, tell me, what have thou done?"

"I raised Hercules to ruin that tree that Bungay raised by his magic spells," Vandermast said.

"Set Hercules to work," Friar Bacon said.

"Now, Hercules, I order thee to return to thy task," Vandermast said. "Pull off the golden branches from the root — the trunk."

"I dare not," the spirit impersonating Hercules said. "Don't thou see great Bacon here, whose frown does more than thy magic can?"

Vandermast told the spirit impersonating Hercules, "By all the thrones, and dominations, virtues, powers, and mighty hierarchies, I order thee to obey Vandermast."

According to Dante's *Divine Comedy*, which in talking about angels follows the ideas of Dionysius the Areopagite, there are three triads of angels, each of which has three orders of angels:

First Triad: The Seraphim, Cherubim, and Thrones.

Second Triad: The Dominations, Virtues, and Powers.

Third Triad: The Principalities, Archangels, and Angels.

The first Triad of Angels consists of the Seraphim, who are associated with the Primum Mobile; the Cherubim, who are associated with the Fixed Stars; and the Thrones, who are associated with Saturn and contemplation.

The second Triad of Angels consists of the Dominations, who are associated with Jupiter and justice; the Virtues, who are associated with Mars and courage; and the Powers, who are associated with the Sun and wisdom.

The third Triad of Angels consists of the Principalities, who are associated with Venus and love; the Archangels, who are associated with Mercury and hope; and the Angels, who are associated with the Moon and faith.

These, of course, are the angels who did not fall with Lucifer.

Also of course, we can put all the Angels in these three groups:

1) The good Angels in Paradise. They are those in the three Triads of Angels.

2) The bad Angels who rebelled with Lucifer. They are under the Moon, in Hell, and are associated with Earth.

3) The neutral Angels who did not take a stand and who are now in the Vestibule of Hell, rejected by both Paradise and the damned souls in Hell. Dante writes about these angels in his *Inferno*.

"Bacon, who bridles and controls headstrong Belcephon, and rules Asmenoth, guider of the north, binds me and prevents me from yielding to Vandermast," the spirit impersonating Hercules said.

"How stands it now, Vandermast?" King Henry III asked. "Have you met your match?"

"Never before was it known to Vandermast that men held devils in such obedient awe," he said. "Bacon does more than ordinary magical art, or else I am mistaken."

"Why, Vandermast, are thou overcome?" the Emperor of Germany said. "Bacon, dispute with him, and test his skill."

"I haven't come, monarchs, in order to hold a debate with such a novice as is Vandermast," Friar Bacon replied. "Instead, I have come to have your royalties — your majesties — to dine with Friar Bacon here in Brazen-nose.

"And, since this German only troubles the place, and holds this audience with a long suspense, I'll send him to his academy and away from here."

The suspense lay in not doing what he — Vandermast — has said he would do: defeat all comers.

Friar Bacon said to the spirit impersonating Hercules, "Thou Hercules, whom Vandermast did raise, transport the German to Hapsburg immediately so that he may learn by travail and travel, in preparation for the spring, more concealed decrees and principles of the magical art."

He added, "Make the tree vanish," and then he said, "Vandermast, thou go away with him!"

The spirit impersonating Hercules exited with Vandermast and the tree.

"Why, Bacon, to where do thou send him?" the Emperor of Germany asked.

"To Hapsburg. There your highness at your return shall find the German safe in his study," Friar Bacon answered.

"Bacon, thou have honored England with thy skill, and made fair Oxford famous by thine art," King Henry III said. "I will be English Henry to thyself and reward you. But tell me, shall we dine with thee today?"

"Yes, with me, my lord, and while I make suitable my cheer — the food and drink I will serve you —"

Seeing Prince Edward approaching, he said, "See where Prince Edward comes to welcome you. He is as gracious as is the morning star of Heaven."

The morning star is the bright planet Venus.

Prince Edward walked into the area, accompanied by Lacy, Warren, and Ermsby.

"Is this Prince Edward, Henry's royal son?" the Emperor of Germany said. "How martial is the character of his face! Yet it is lovely and beset with amorets."

Amorets are looks that inspire love.

"Ned, where have thou been?" King Henry III asked.

"At Fremingham, my lord, to test your bucks to see if they could escape the teasers or the toil," Prince Edward replied.

In this culture, male deer were called bucks. The teasers were hunting dogs that were trained to rouse the game. A toil was a net.

Prince Edward continued, "But hearing that these lordly potentates had landed and traveled up to Oxford town, I rode to give a welcome to them. Especially the German monarch, but next to him, and joined with him, the King of Castile and the Duke of Saxony are as welcome as they may be to the English court. So much for the men — but see, the goddess of beauty, Venus, appears, or one who surpasses Venus in her form! Sweet Eleanor, who makes the goddess of beauty swell with pride, and who is rich nature's glory and her wealth at one and the same time, beauty of all beauties, welcome to Albion — England. Welcome to me, and welcome to thine own, if thou will condescend to accept the welcome from myself."

Eleanor replied, "Martial Plantagenet, Henry's high-minded son, the target at which Eleanor aimed, I liked thee before I saw thee; now I love thee as much as in so short a time I may, yet I love thee so much that time shall never break that love, and therefore so accept Eleanor."

"Fear not, my lord," the King of Castile said to King Edward III. "This couple will agree, if love may creep into their playful eyes."

He then said to Prince Edward, "And therefore, Edward, I accept thee here, as my adopted son, thereby preventing any suspense."

Prince Edward and Eleanor were to marry, and their fathers supported their match.

King Henry III said, "Let me who takes joy in these harmonious greetings, and glory in these honors done to Ned, my son, yield thanks for all these favors to my son, and I will remain a true Plantagenet to all."

Miles arrived, carrying a tablecloth and trenchers and a salt-cellar. A trencher is a wooden plate; royal persons would expect to use more expensive plates.

Miles said:

"*Salvete, omnes reges*,

["Hail, all kings,]

"Who govern your *greges* [flocks]

"In Saxony and Spain,

"In England and in Almain [Germany]!

"For all this frolic rabble [merry mob]

"Must I cover the table

"With trenchers, salt, and cloth [tablecloth];

"And then look for your broth."

"What pleasant — merry — fellow is this?" the Emperor of Germany asked about Miles.

"He is, my lord, Doctor Bacon's poor scholar," King Henry III answered.

Miles said to himself, "My master has made me sewer of these great lords; and, God knows, I am as good at service at a table as a sow is under an apple-tree."

The only thing a sow under an apple-tree is good for is eating apples. Miles was also good at eating.

Miles continued talking to himself, "It does not matter; their food and drink shall not be great, and therefore what does it matter where the salt-cellar stands, at the top or at the bottom of the table?

A "sewer" is the servant who sets the table for a meal.

Salt was expensive, so it was placed close to those diners who had the most status and who were seated at the top of the table.

Miles exited.

"These scholars know more skill in axioms, and how to use quips and sleights of tongue of sophistry, than how to set a table correctly for a king," the King of Castile said.

Miles returned with pottage and broth; Friar Bacon followed him.

Friar Bacon had criticized Miles for spilling the food, which Miles was denying.

"Spill, sir? Why, do you think I never carried two-penny chop before in my life?" Miles said.

"Twopenny chop" is an inexpensive food that contains chopped meat.

Miles then said to the Emperor of Germany:

"By your leave, *nobile decus* [noble crown, aka noble person],

"For here comes Doctor Bacon's *pecus* [beast],

"Being in his full age

["Being old enough]

"To carry a mess of pottage."

Twopenny chop, pottage, and broth were lowly fare — definitely not the kind of food and drink that the Emperor of Germany was accustomed to be served.

Friar Bacon said, "Lordings, do not marvel that your food is this, for we at Oxford must keep to our plain academic fare. There must be no riotous living where philosophy reigns. So therefore, Henry, assign places to these potentates, and bid them to fall to and eat their frugal 'delicacies.'"

"Presumptuous, arrogant friar!" the Emperor of Germany complained. "What, do thou scoff at a king? What, do thou taunt us with thy peasants' fare, and give us 'delicacies' fit for country swains?"

He then said to King Henry III, "Henry, does this jest proceed with thy consent, to twit us with a pittance of such low value? Tell me, and I, Frederick the Second, will not grieve thee long — I won't trouble you with my presence."

"By Henry's honor, and the royal faith that the English monarch bears to his friend, I knew not of the friar's feeble fare, nor am I pleased he entertains you thus," King Henry III said.

"Be calm, Frederick, for I showed these 'delicacies' to you to let thee see how scholars are accustomed to eat and how little food refines our English wits," Friar Bacon said to the Emperor of Germany.

He then ordered, "Miles, take it away, and let it be thy dinner."

"Indeed, sir, I will," Miles said. "This day shall be a festival-day with me, for I shall exceed in the highest degree the usual amount of food I eat. Today, I will feast as if it were a holiday."

He exited, carrying away the plain food and drink.

Friar Bacon said to the Emperor of Germany, "I tell thee, monarch, all the German peers could not afford to entertain you — so royal and so full of majesty — in such a way as Bacon will present to Frederick.

"The humblest waiter who attends to and fills thy goblets shall be in honors greater than thyself."

The word "honors" may mean "outward show," or Friar Bungay may have subtly insulted the Emperor of Germany.

Friar Bungay continued, "And as for thy delicacies, rich spices from Alexandria, fetched by caravels — light ships — from Egypt's richest straits, found in the wealthy regions of Africa, shall make royal the table of my king. Wines richer than those the Egyptian courtesan — Cleopatra — drank to Caesar Augustus' kingly rival — Mark Antony — shall be caroused in English Henry's feast."

Cleopatra once bet Mark Antony that she could consume a meal worth 10 million sesterces. She won the bet by dissolving a pearl worth 10 million sesterces in wine and then drinking the wine.

Friar Bacon continued, "Crete shall yield the richest of her sugar; Persia, down her Volga by canoes, shall send down the secrets of her spices."

Friar Bacon may have known magic, but he did not know geography. The Volga River is in Russia.

Friar Bacon continued, "The African dates; mirabolans, aka dried plums, of Spain; conserves, aka fruit preserved in sugar; and suckets, aka candied fruit, from Tiberias in Galilee; delicacies from Judea, choicer than the lamps

— torches and lamprey eels — that fired Rome with sparks of gluttony, shall beautify the table for Frederick.

"And therefore you need not complain about a friar's feast."

CHAPTER 10

— Scene 10 —

In Fressingfield, the country squires Lambert and Serlsby talked with the gamekeeper.

Lambert said, "Come, frolicsome gamekeeper of our liege's game, whose table laden with food always has venison and blackjacks — leather jugs — of wine to welcome travelers, know that I'm in love with jolly Margaret, who outshines our damsels as the Moon darkens by comparison the brightest sparkles — the stars — of the night. In the village of Laxfield here, my land and income lie. I'll make thy daughter jointer of it all, provided that thou consent to give her to me to be my wife. I can spend five hundred marks a year — that's my income."

By making her jointer, he meant that Margaret would inherit all he had if he predeceased her. They would hold the property in joint possession.

Five hundred marks a year is a good income.

Serlsby said, "I am the landlord, gamekeeper, of thy property. I own the land on which you make your income; people in Laxfield have never seen me raise the rent I charge. I will enfeoff — give ownership to — fair Margaret in all, as long as she will take herself to a vigorous squire — me — and marry me."

The gamekeeper replied to the two suitors for Margaret, "Now, courteous gentlemen, if the gamekeeper's girl has pleased the liking fancy of you both, and with her beauty has subdued your thoughts, it is uncertain how to decide the question of whom she should marry.

"It makes me joyful that such men of great reputation and worth should lay their liking and preference on a person of this base estate, and it makes me joyful that her situation in life should grow so fortunate to have her be a wife to meaner men than you, much less men as great as you two.

"But since such squires will stoop to a gamekeeper's social status and marry a gamekeeper's daughter, I will, to avoid displeasing either of you, call Margaret forth, and she shall make her choice."

"Agreed, gamekeeper," Lambert said. "Send her to us."

The gamekeeper exited to get his daughter.

Lambert said, "Why, Serlsby, thy wife is so recently dead. Has all thy love for her so lightly passed over and been forgotten that thou can wed before the year is out?"

"I don't live, Lambert, to make the dead content, nor was I wedded to her except for life," Serlsby replied. "The grave ends and begins a married state."

A wife's death ends the marriage, but leaves the widower free to remarry.

Margaret entered the scene.

Seeing her, Lambert said, "Peggy, the lovely flower of all towns, Suffolk's own beautiful Helen of Troy, and rich England's star, whose beauty, mixed with her housewife's skills, makes all England talk of merry Fressingfield!"

Serlsby said, "I cannot fancify my language with poesies, nor paint my passions with comparisons, nor tell a tale of Phoebus Apollo and his loves. But believe me when I say this: Laxfield here is mine, of long-established rent seven-hundred pounds each year, and if thou can but love a country squire, I will enfeoff thee, Margaret, and grant possession of all of it to thee. I cannot flatter, but test me, if thou please."

"Excellent neighboring squires, the foundations of Suffolk's region, a gamekeeper's daughter is too base and low in social degree to marry men accounted of such worth," Margaret said to her two suitors. "But if I would not displease one of you, I would reply."

"Give us your answer, Peggy," Lambert said. "No answer shall make us discontent."

His statement was ambiguous. It could mean 1) If you do not answer, it shall make us discontent, or 2) No matter what you answer, it shall not make us discontent.

"Then, gentlemen, note that love has little permanence, nor can the flames that Venus sets on fire be kindled except but by fancy's stirring of emotion," Margaret said. "So then give me pardon, gentlemen, if a maiden's reply is uncertain, until I have debated with myself whom love shall make me favor."

"Let it be me," Serlsby said, "and trust me, Margaret, the meadows surrounded with the silver streams, whose nourishing pastures fatten all my flocks, yielding forth fleeces with such long-haired, good-quality wool that the wool-famous town of Lempster cannot yield finer stuff, and forty cattle with fair and burnished — gleaming — heads, with swollen udders that hang down to the ground, shall serve thy dairy, if thou wed me."

"Forget about the country wealth, such as flocks and cattle, and lands that wave with the golden sheaves of Ceres, the goddess of agriculture, filling my barns with the plenty of the fields," Lambert said. "But, Peggy, if thou wed thyself to me, thou shall have garments of embroidered silk, fabric of fine lawn, and rich interlaced fabrics for thy head-attire: Costly shall be thy beautiful clothing, if thou will just be Lambert's loving wife."

"Be content, gentlemen, you have offered fair inducements for me to marry you, and more than is suitable for a country maiden's degree," Margaret said. "But give me permission to think about this for a time, for love blooms not at the first assault. Give me just ten days to think about it, and I will reply and tell you which or to whom I myself affectionates — have affection and love for."

"Lambert, I tell thee, thou are importunate," Serlsby said. "Such beauty is not suitable for such a lowly country esquire: It is for Serlsby to have Margaret."

"Do thou think with wealth to overreach and rise above me?" Lambert said. "Serlsby, I scorn to endure thy country boasts. I dare thee, coward, to maintain this wrong, by dint of rapier, single in the field. Let's duel, one on one, in the field."

"I'll back up, Lambert, what I have avouched," Serlsby said.

He then said, "Margaret, farewell; another time shall serve."

He exited.

"I'll follow you," Lambert said.

He then said, "Peggy, farewell to thyself. Listen how well I'll fight for thy love."

He exited.

"How Lady Fortune mixes lucky happenings with frowns, and wrongs me with the sweets of my delight!" Margaret said. "She wrongs me with what delighted me! Love is my bliss, and love is now my bale — my woe. Shall I be like Helen of Troy in my harsh fates, as I am like her in my unmatched beauty, and set rich Suffolk with my face afire?"

Helen of Troy's beauty had caused Prince Paris of Troy and King Menelaus of Sparta to come into conflict, and now Margaret's beauty was causing Lambert and Serlsby to fight a duel.

She continued, "If lovely Lacy were but with his Peggy, the cloudy darkness of Lacy's bitter frown would put a stop to the pride of these aspiring squires. Before the term of ten days has expired, when they look for a reply about their loves, my lord will come to merry Fressingfield, and end the fancies and the follies of both of them. Until then, Peggy, be blithe and merry and of good cheer."

A post-messenger arrived; he was carrying a letter and a bag of gold. Post-messengers ride on horseback to quickly deliver letters and messages and parcels.

"Fair lovely damsel, which way does this path lead?" the post-messenger asked. "How might I most quickly go to Fressingfield? Which footpath leads to the gamekeeper's lodge?"

"Your way is straight ahead, and this path is right," Margaret said. "I myself dwell by here in Fressingfield, and if the gamekeeper is the man you seek, I am his daughter. May I know the cause of your errand?"

The post-messenger said to himself, "She is lovely, and once beloved by my lord. No marvel if his eye was lodged so low, when brighter beauty does not exist in the Heavens."

He then said out loud, "The Earl of Lincoln has sent you a letter here, and, with it, exactly a hundred pounds in gold."

He gave her the letter and the moneybag and said, "Sweet, bonny, pretty wench, read the letter, and give me a reply I can take back to Lord Lacy."

"The scrolls that Jove sent Danae, wrapped in rich coverings of fine shining gold, were not more welcome than these lines to me," Margaret said. "Tell me, while I break the seals of this letter, does Lacy live well? How fares my lovely lord?"

"Yes, he lives well, if wealth may make men live well," the post-messenger said.

Margaret read the letter out loud:

"The blossoms of the almond-tree grow in a night, and vanish in a morning; the flies known as ephemerae, fair Peggy, take life with the Sun, and die with the dew — they live for only a day. Love that slips in with a gaze, goes out with a wink; and too hasty loves have always the shortest length. I write this as the one who causes thy grief, and as the one who is my folly, the one who at Fressingfield loved that which time has taught me to be but mean and lowly dainties: Eyes are dissemblers, and love is but queasy and fickle; therefore, know, Margaret, that I have chosen a Spanish lady to be my wife. She is the chief waiting-woman to the Princess Eleanor; she is a fair lady, and no less beautiful than thyself, and she is

*highly born and wealthy. In that I forsake thee, I leave thee to thine own liking —
you are free to marry any other man you choose; and for thy dowry I have sent thee
a hundred pounds; and always assure thee of my favor, which shall benefit thee and
thine much.*

"Farewell.

"Not thine, nor his own, for I belong to another,

"Edward Lacy."

Margaret said, "Foolish Ate, goddess of catastrophe and giver of bad-boding destinies, the goddess that wraps proud fortune in thy snaky locks, did thou enchant my birthday with such stars as flashed mischief like lightning from their infancy at the beginning of time? If the Heavens had vowed, if stars had made decree, to show on me their astrological perverse influence, and if Lacy had but loved, then the Heavens, Hell, and all, could not have wronged the patience of my mind."

"It grieves me, damsel," the post-messenger said, "but the earl is forced to love the lady by King Henry the Third's command."

"Not all the wealth combined within the English shores, nor Europe's commander, nor the English king, would have moved the love of Peggy away from her lord," Margaret replied.

Europe's commander is the Holy Roman Emperor.

"What answer shall I return to my lord?" the post-messenger asked.

"First, because thou came from Lacy whom I loved — ah, give me permission to sigh at the very thought! — take, my friend, the hundred pounds he sent because what Margaret has resolved to do needs no dowry," she replied. "The world shall be regarded by her as worthless vanity; wealth shall be regarded by her as trash; love shall be regarded by her as hate; pleasure shall be regarded by her as despair. For I will immediately go to stately Fremingham, and in the abbey there be shorn — made — a nun, and yield my loves and liberty to God."

Nuns often had their hair chopped short as a way of renouncing vanity and worldly things.

She continued, "Fellow, I give thee this, not for the news you gave me, for that news is hateful to Margaret, but because thou serve Lacy, who was once Margaret's love."

"What I have heard, what passions I have seen, I'll report them to the earl," the post-messenger said.

Margaret replied, "Say that she is happy that his love has settled on one person, and she prays that his misfortune may be hers."

Margaret's final words were ambiguous: 1) She prays that Lacy, who rejected her, is in turn rejected by his new love, or 2) She prays that any misfortune that may fall on Lacy will fall on her instead.

CHAPTER 11

In his cell, Friar Bacon lay on a bed, with a white stick — his wand — in one hand, a book in the other, and a lamp lighted beside him. The Brazen Head was in his cell. Miles, who was armed with pistols and a brown bill (a halberd painted brown), walked over to him.

Friar Bacon had worked for seven years to create the Brazen Head, which he hoped would speak and tell him truths unknown to Humankind. For 60 days, he and Friar Bungay had taken shifts to watch the Brazen Head. Now it was almost ready to speak.

"Miles, where are you?" Friar Bacon called.

"Here, sir," Miles answered.

"Why did you tarry so long?"

"Do you think that watching the Brazen Head demands no weapons? I promise you, sir, I have armed myself like this so that if all your devils come, I will not fear them even an inch — even a tiny bit."

"Miles, thou know that I have dived into Hell, and sought the darkest palaces of fiends," Friar Bacon said. "Thou know that on account of my magic spells great Belcephon has left his lodging in Hell and kneeled at my cell. Thou know that the rafters of the earth were torn from the poles, and three-formed Luna hid her silver looks, trembling upon her concave continent, the crescent Moon, when Bacon read upon his magic book."

Three goddesses were associated with Luna the Moon: Selene (Roman name: Luna) in the Heavens, Artemis (Roman name: Diana) on Earth, and Hecate in the Underworld. Thus Friar Bacon called Luna "three-formed."

Friar Bacon continued, "With seven years of tossing necromantic charms, poring upon and studying the principles of dark Hecate, goddess of witchcraft, I have created a monstrous Head of Brass that, by the enchanting forces of the devil, shall speak strange and unknown aphorisms, and shall surround fair England with a wall of brass. Bungay and I have kept watch for these threescore — sixty — days, and now our vital spirits crave some rest. Even if Argus lived, and had his hundred eyes, they could not watch during Phobetor's night."

Friar Bacon was saying that this night, all of Argos' one hundred eyes would sleep.

Argus was a watchman for Juno, the goddess wife of the god Jupiter. Because he had so many eyes, some could sleep while the others stayed awake. Zeus sent Hermes to kill Argus. He accomplished this by playing music to first put all one hundred of Argus' eyes to sleep.

Phobetor was the son of Somnus, the god of sleep. Phobetor brought nightmares to sleepers. His brother, Morpheus, is the god of dreams.

Friar Bacon continued, "Now, Miles, in thee rests Friar Bacon's well-being: The honor and renown of all his life hangs in the watching of this Brazen Head. Therefore, I order thee by the immortal God, Who holds the souls of men within His fist, that this night thou stay awake and keep watch, for before the morning star sends out his glorious glistering on the north, the Head will speak. At that time, Miles, upon thy life, awaken me; for then by magic art I'll work to end my seven years' task with excellence. If thou shut thy watchful eye for only a wink, then farewell to Bacon's glory and his fame! Draw close the curtains, Miles. Now, on thy life, be watchful, and ...."

Friar Bacon fell asleep.

"So," Miles said. "I thought you would talk yourself asleep soon, and it is no wonder, for Bungay during the days, and he during the nights, have watched just these ten and fifty days. Now this is the night they have waited for, and it is my task, and no more. Now, Jesus bless me, what a splendid Brazen Head it is! And what a splendid nose! You talk of *nos autem glorificare*, but here's a nose that I promise may be called *nos autem populare* for the people of the parish."

The Latin "*nos autem glorificare*" may mean "moreover, to glorify us."

The Latin "*nos autem populare*" is possibly untranslatable or Miles may have meant it to mean "moreover, a popular nose," knowing that Miles is punning on "*nos*" as "nose."

Miles was parodying the Introit for the Maundy Thursday Evening Mass, which begins:

"*Nos autem gloriari oportet in Cruce Domini nostri Iesu Christi ....*"

Translated, this means: "We are to glory in the cross of our Lord Jesus Christ ...."

Since Miles is punning on "*nos*" and "nose," chances are good that "*nostri*" reminded him of "nostrils."

Miles continued, "Well, I am furnished with weapons. Now, sir, I will set me down by a post, and make it as good as a watchman to wake me, if I should happen to slumber."

He positioned himself in such a way that if he dropped off to sleep, his head would hit the post and wake him.

He continued, "I thought, Goodman Head, I would call you out of your memento."

By "memento," Miles meant "daydream" or "reverie," but if the Brazen Head were a brass skull, it would be a *memento mori*.

Miles drifted off to sleep, and his head hit the post, waking him.

He cried, "By the passion of God, I have almost broken my head!"

A great noise sounded.

"Up, Miles, go to your task," Miles said to himself. "Take your brown-bill in your hand; here's some of your master's hobgoblins abroad."

The Brazen Head spoke: "Time is."

In other words, "It is time."

For one thing, it is time for Miles to awaken Friar Bacon. For another, it is time for the Brazen Head to reveal truths unknown to Humankind.

Miles said, "'Time is!' Why, Master Brazen Head, have you such a capital nose, and yet you answer with syllables: 'Time is'? Is this all my master's cunning can do: to spend seven years' study about 'Time is'? Well, sir, it may be we shall have some better orations from it soon. Well, I'll watch you as narrowly as ever you were watched, and I'll play with you as the nightingale played with the slow-worm; I'll set a prick against my breast. Now rest there, Miles."

Nightingales were thought to sing while their breast leaned against a thorn. This kept them awake and able to sing songs to the slow-worm, a small, legless, burrowing lizard. This time, Miles positioned himself leaning against his halberd, which would prick and awaken him if he fell asleep.

Miles fell asleep, but he was awakened by the prick of his halberd and said, "Lord, have mercy upon me! I have almost killed myself!"

A great noise sounded.

"Up, Miles. Listen how they rumble," Miles said to himself.

The Brazen Head spoke: "Time was."

"Well, Friar Bacon, you have spent your seven years' study 'well,' in that you can make your head speak but two words at one time: 'Time was.' Yes, indeed, a time was when my master was a wise man, but that was before he began to make the Brazen Head. You, Friar Bacon, shall lie asleep until your arse aches if your Brazen Head speaks no better than this. Well, I will watch, and walk up and down, and be a Peripatetian and a philosopher of Aristotle's stamp."

Aristotle's students were called Peripatetics because they followed Aristotle, who taught as he walked. Because Miles kept falling asleep and hurting himself, he sought to stay awake by walking around the room.

A great noise sounded.

"What, a fresh noise? Take thy pistols in hand, Miles."

He drew his pistols.

The Brazen Head spoke: "Time is past."

Lightning flashed, and a hand appeared and broke the Brazen Head with a hammer.

"Master, master, get up!" Miles shouted. "Hell's broken loose; your Head speaks; and there's such a thunder and lightning that I promise you all Oxford is up in arms. Get out of your bed, and take a brown-bill in your hand; the latter day — the Judgment Day — has come."

Friar Bacon got up and said, "Miles, I am coming."

Not knowing that the Brazen Head had been broken, he said to Miles, 'Oh, surpassingly warily watched! Bacon will make thee next himself in love. I will love you almost as much as I love myself. "

Seeing the broken pieces of the Brazen Head, he asked, "When did the Head speak?"

"When did the Head speak!" Miles said. "Didn't you say that the Head would tell strange principles of philosophy? Why, sir, it speaks only two words at a time."

"Why, villain, has it spoken often?" Friar Bacon asked.

"Often!" Miles said. "Yes, marry, it has, thrice; but in all those three times it has uttered only seven words."

"What did it say?"

"Indeed, sir, the first time he said, "Time is,' as if Fabius Commentator should have pronounced a sentence."

Quintus Fabius Maximus Verrucosus was a Roman general who opposed the great Carthaginian general Hannibal after Hannibal and his army crossed the Alps and reached Italy. Because Hannibal's army had won important victories and crushed the Roman soldiers opposing him, Fabius did not meet him in open battle, but instead followed and harassed him, giving the Romans time to recover from their losses. Because of this successful tactic, he was given the nickname "Cunctator," which means "the Delayer." Miles himself had delayed in waking up Friar Bacon.

Miles continued, "The second time he said, 'Time was,' and the third time, with thunder and lightning, as if he were very angry, he said, 'Time is past.'"

"It is past indeed!" Friar Bacon said, looking at the broken pieces of the Brazen Head. "Ah, villain! Time is past. My life, my fame, my glory, all are past. Bacon, the turrets — the high points — of thy hope are ruined down, thy seven years of study lie in the dust. Thy Brazen Head lies broken through a slave who watched and would not call me when the Head wanted you to call me."

He then asked Miles, "What did the Head say first?"

"Even, sir, 'Time is.'"

"Villain, if thou would have called to me, Bacon, then, if thou would have watched, and waked the sleepy friar, the Brazen Head would have uttered unknown principles, and England would have been encircled with a wall of brass. But proud Asmenoth, ruler of the north, and Demogorgon, master of the fates, resent that a mortal man should be able to accomplish so much. Hell trembled at my deep-commanding spells, and fiends frowned to see a man their superior. Bacon could have boasted more than any other man could boast! But now the boasts of Bacon have come to an end, and Europe's favorable opinion of Bacon has come to an end. His seven years of work have come to a bad ending. And, villain, since my glory has come to an end, I will appoint thee to some fatal and deadly end. Villain, avoid — leave! Get thee out of Bacon's sight! Vagrant, go roam and range and wander about the world, and perish as a vagabond on earth!"

Matthew 4:10 states, "*Then said Jesus unto him, Avoid[,] Satan: for it is written, Thou shalt worship the Lord thy God, and him only shalt thou serve*" (1599 Geneva Bible).

"Avoid, Satan" means "Leave, Satan."

"Why, then, sir, do you forbid me to continue in your service?" Miles asked.

"My service, villain! I do so with a fatal curse that direful and terrible plagues and mischief fall on thee."

"It doesn't matter. I am ahead of you with this old proverb: The more the fox is cursed, the better he fares."

He was punning on "cursed," or "coursed," and "fares," which can mean "go": The more the fox is pursued, the better he goes.

Miles continued, "God be with you, sir. I'll take just a book in my hand, dress like a scholar with a wide-sleeved gown on my back and a crowned academic cap on my head, and see if I can want a promotion."

The word "want" means "lack." Perhaps Miles should have used the word "get." Or perhaps he meant that it would be difficult for him not to get a promotion.

Friar Bacon said, "May some fiend or ghost haunt and pursue thy weary steps, until the fiends and ghosts transport thee alive to Hell, for Bacon shall never have a merry day because he has lost the fame and honor of his Brazen Head."

CHAPTER 12

At the court, the Emperor of Germany, the King of Castile, King Henry III, Princess Eleanor, Prince Edward, Lacy, and Ralph Simnell the Jester met.

The Emperor of Germany asked Prince Edward, "Now, lovely prince, the prime example of Albion's wealth, how fare the Lady Eleanor and you? Have you courted and found Castile qualified to answer England in equivalence? Will there be a match — a marriage — between bonny, pretty Nell and thee?"

Prince Edward answered rhetorically, "Could Paris enter the courts of Greece, and not become imprisoned by fair Helen's looks? Or could Phoebus Apollo escape those piercing love-inducing looks of Daphne when she glanced at his deity?"

The answer to these questions, of course, is no.

He added, "Can Edward, then, sit by a flame — a flame of beauty whose heat surpasses that of Helen and fair Daphne — and freeze? Now, monarchs, ask the lady if we are in agreement."

"Madam, has my son found favor with you?" King Henry III asked.

"Seeing, my lord, his lovely portrait, and hearing how his mind agreed with his lovely shape, I came from Spain, traveling with all this warlike retinue, and not uncertain about loving him, but already so affectionate that Edward has in England what he had already won from me while I was still in Spain," Eleanor replied.

"A match and a marriage, my lord!" the King of Castile said. "These 'wantons' can't help but love each other!"

He was using the word "wantons" affectionately.

He continued, "Men must have wives, and women will be wed. Let's hasten the day on which we will honor the marriage rites. Let's have the wedding earlier rather than later."

Ralph the Jester asked, "Sirrah Harry, shall Ned marry Nell?"

"Yes, Ralph," King Henry III said. "What about it?"

"Indeed, Harry, follow my advice," Ralph the Jester replied. "Send for Friar Bacon to marry them, for he'll so conjure him and her with his necromancy that they shall love together like pig and lamb while they live."

Ralph the Jester seemed to be saying that a magical spell would be needed for the two to be happily married, but since pig and lamb usually don't love together, he may have really been saying that even with a magical spell Prince Edward and Eleanor would not have a happy marriage. But pig and lamb together make a feast, and so perhaps he was saying that a cornucopia of happiness lay ahead for the couple.

"But listen, Ralph," the King of Castile said. "Are thou happy to have Eleanor as thy lady boss?"

"Yes, as long as she will promise me two things," Ralph the Jester replied.

"What are they, Ralph?" the King of Castile asked.

"That she will never scold Ned, nor fight with me," Ralph the Jester answered.

He then said to King Henry III, "Sirrah Harry, I have put one over on Eleanor by giving her a thing impossible to do."

"What's that, Ralph?" King Henry III asked.

"Why, Harry, did thou ever see a woman who could restrain both her tongue and her hands? No. But when egg-pies grow on apple-trees — something that is impossible — then will thy grey mare prove to be a bagpiper."

According to the proverb "the grey mare is the better horse," the wife always dominates the husband. A bagpiper needs to control both the tongue and the hands. Ralph the Jester was saying that it was impossible for Eleanor to exhibit such control.

The King of Castile and Lacy had been talking quietly together during Ralph the Jester's comic talk.

The Emperor of Germany asked them, "Why are the Lord of Castile and the Earl of Lincoln engaged in such earnest and private talk?"

"I stand, my lord, amazed at Lacy's talk," the King of Castile said. "I am amazed at how he speaks at length of the constancy and faithfulness about one surnamed, because of her beauty's excellence, the Fair Maiden of merry Fressingfield."

"It is true, my lord," King Henry III said. "It is wondrous to hear. Her beauty surpasses that of Mars' paramour. Her right to be called a virgin is as rich — deserved — as Vesta's is. Lacy and Ned have told me miraculous things about her beauty."

Mars' paramour is Venus, goddess of beauty, with whom he had an affair.

Vesta is a virgin goddess. The three virgin goddesses of the Romans also included Minerva and Diana. Their Greek names were Hestia, Athena, and Artemis.

"What does Lord Lacy say?" the King of Castile asked. "Shall she be his wife?"

Lacy was supposed to be engaged to marry the chief waiting-woman to the Princess Eleanor, but the King of Castile did not mind if Lacy married the Fair Maiden of merry Fressingfield.

"Or else Lord Lacy is unfit to live," Lacy replied.

He then asked King Henry III, "May it please your highness to give me permission to ride posthaste to Fressingfield? I'll fetch the bonny, pretty girl, and prove, by her true appearance at the court, what I have declared often with my tongue."

If the King of Castile did not mind if Lacy married the Fair Maiden of merry Fressingfield, then King Henry III did not mind, either. At least, not much.

"Lacy, go to the equerry who takes care of the horses in my stable, and take such coursers as shall suit thy purpose," King Henry III said. "Hurry thee to Fressingfield, and bring home the lass; and, because her fame flies through the English land, if it may please the lady Eleanor" — he turned and faced her and said to her — "one day shall match your excellence and hers. Two marriages will be performed on that day: yours and that of the Fair Maiden of Fressingfield."

King Henry III may have been peeved enough at Lacy's not marrying the woman he had ordered him to marry that he wanted the marriage of the gamekeeper's daughter to take place on the same day and at the same place as the marriage of the King of Castile's daughter. Fortunately, Princess Eleanor rose to the occasion.

"We Castile ladies are not very aloof," Eleanor said. "Your highness may command a greater boon than that. And glad am I to grace the Lincoln Earl by being the partner of his marriage day. Two weddings will be performed on that day."

"Great thanks, Nell, for I love the lord Lacy, as he who is second to thyself in love," Prince Edward said.

His last words were ambiguous and could mean 1) I love Lacy second to you, Eleanor, and/or 2) His love for the Fair Maiden of Fressingfield is second to my love for you, Eleanor.

"You love her?" Ralph the Jester asked.

He then said to Eleanor, "Madam Nell, never believe that Prince Edward loves you, although he swears he loves you."

"Why, Ralph?" Eleanor asked.

"Why, his love is like a tavern-keeper's mirror that is broken with every touch; for he loved the Fair Maiden of Fressingfield once out of all moderation," Ralph the Jester replied.

He then said to Prince Edward, who was frowning at him, "Nay, Ned, never send significant looks at me; I don't care, I."

Prince Edward's significant looks meant, Knock it off! Don't tell the woman I am going to marry that I loved another woman!

"Ralph tells all," King Henry III said to Prince Edward. "You shall have a 'good' secretary in him."

Secretaries are confidants who are entrusted with secrets, and so King Henry III was joking when he said that Ralph the Jester would make a good secretary.

King Henry III added, "But, Lacy, hasten thee posthaste to Fressingfield, for before thou have prepared all things for her rise in social status, the ceremonial marriage day will be at hand."

"I go, my lord," Lacy said.

He exited.

The Emperor of Germany asked King Henry III, "How shall we pass this day, my lord?"

"On horse, my lord," he replied. "The day is surpassingly fair. We'll flush the partridge from cover, or go rouse the deer. Follow, my lords; you shall not lack for sport and entertainment."

CHAPTER 13

— Scene 13 —

Friar Bacon was sitting in his cell when Friar Bungay came to visit him.

Friar Bungay asked, "Why is the friar who frolicked so recently now sitting as melancholy and apathetic in his cell as if he had neither lost nor won today?"

He knew that the Brazen Head was supposed to have spoken by now, and he knew that Friar Bacon looked dejected and unable to take any action. Of course, Friar Bacon was upset about the breaking of the Brazen Head, but something else was also bothering him.

"Ah, Bungay, my Brazen Head is spoiled, my glory gone, my seven years' study lost!" Friar Bacon said. "The fame of Bacon, bruited and proclaimed throughout the world, shall end and perish with this deep disgrace."

"Bacon has built the foundation of his fame so securely on the wings of true report by performing strange and unaccustomed miracles that this cannot destroy what he deserves," Friar Bungay said.

"Bungay, sit down, for by my skill in foretelling the future I find that this day shall fall out ominously," Friar Bacon said. "Some deadly act shall befall me before I sleep, but what and wherein I cannot guess."

"My mind is heavy, whatsoever shall happen," Friar Bungay said.

A knock sounded.

"Who is knocking?" Friar Bacon asked.

After opening the door and looking out, Friar Bungay replied, "It's two scholars who desire to speak with you."

"Tell them to come in," Friar Bacon said.

The two scholars entered Friar Bacon's cell.

"Now, my youths, what do you want?" Friar Bacon asked.

The first scholar said, "Sir, we are men from Suffolk, and we are neighboring friends. Our fathers are vigorous squires in their countries. Their lands adjoin: My father dwells in Crackfield, and his father dwells in Laxfield. We are students in the same college, and we are sworn brothers, as our fathers live as friends."

"Why are you telling me all this?" Friar Bacon asked.

The second scholar said, "Hearing your worship kept within your cell a magic mirror with a far-seeing prospective, wherein men might see whatsoever their thoughts or hearts' desire could wish, we come to know how our fathers are faring."

"My magic mirror is free for every honest man," Friar Bacon said. "Sit down, and you shall see before long how or in what state your friendly fathers live. Meanwhile, tell me your names."

The first scholar said, "Mine is Lambert, Junior."

The second scholar said, "And mine is Serlsby, Junior."

"Bungay, I smell there will be a tragedy," Friar Bacon said.

In the mirror, the two students' fathers, Lambert and Serlsby, appeared. They were ready to fight a duel with rapiers and daggers. Each would use his rapier to attack the other, and each would use his dagger to parry the attacks of the other.

Lambert said, "Serlsby, thou have kept thine hour and showed up like a man at the hour appointed for our duel: You are worthy of the title of a squire — you dare to show thy love for thy loved one and thy desire for thy loved one's favor by risking thy blood and life.

"Thou know what words passed between us at Fressingfield: They were such shameless insults as manhood cannot endure — yes, for I scorn to bear such piercing taunts. Prepare thyself, Serlsby; one of us will die."

"Thou see I single thee the field," Serlsby said.

He was using hunting terminology: Hunters would often separate a single deer from the herd and then kill it.

He continued, "And what I spoke, I'll maintain its truth with my sword. Stand on thy guard for I cannot settle this quarrel with talk. If thou kill me, remember that I have a son who lives in Oxford in the Broadgates Hall and who will revenge his father's blood with blood."

"And, Serlsby, I have at Oxford a vigorous boy who dares with weapons to fight thy son and lives in Broadgates Hall, too, as well as thine," Lambert replied. "But draw thy rapier, for we'll have a bout of fighting."

Friar Bacon moved aside to let the two scholars see into the magic mirror without obstruction and said, "Now, vigorous young gentlemen, look within the magic mirror, and tell me if you can discern your sires."

"Serlsby, it is hard; thy father acts wrongly when he combats my father in the field," Lambert, Jr., said.

"Lambert, Jr., thou lie," Serlsby, Jr., said. "My father is the abused, wronged party, and thou shall find that what I say is true, if my father suffers harm."

This culture believed that a fight could settle the truth of a statement because God would help the person who told the truth to win.

"How goes it, sirs?" Friar Bungay asked. "What is happening?"

"Our fathers are in combat near Fressingfield," Lambert, Jr., said.

"Sit still, my friends, and see the outcome," Friar Bacon said.

In the mirror, Lambert said, "Why do thou just stand there, Serlsby? Are thou afraid for thy life? A veney, man! Let's fight! Beautiful Margaret craves for us to fight."

"A veney" is a fencing term meaning "a bout."

"Then this for her," Serlsby said.

They began to duel.

"Ah, well thrust!" Lambert, Jr., said.

"But see the defensive parry," Serlsby, Jr., said.

Their fathers fought and inflicted mortal wounds on each other.

"Oh, I am slain!" Lambert said.

He died.

"And I am slain," Serlsby said. "Lord, have mercy on me!"

He died.

"My father is slain!" Lambert, Jr., said. "Serlsby, Jr., defend against that."

He lashed out at him with his dagger.

"And my father is slain!" Serlsby, Jr., said. "Lambert, Jr., I'll repay thee well."

The two scholars stabbed each other, and died.

"Oh, what a violent outcome!" Friar Bungay said.

Looking in the mirror, Friar Bacon said, "See, Friar Bungay, where the fathers both lie dead!"

He then looked at the slain youths and said, "Bacon, thy magic effected this massacre: This magic mirror works many woes."

The magic mirror did not cause the death of the fathers, but by allowing the sons to see their fathers' death, it was a cause of the anger that made the two sons kill each other.

Friar Bacon continued, "And therefore seeing that these brave vigorous brutes — heroes — these youths who were friends, have perished because of thine art, thou, Bacon, must end all thy magic and thine art at once. The dagger that ended their doomed lives shall break the *cause efficiat* of their woes."

According to legend, the first King of Britain was the Trojan Brutus, who founded Troynovant — New Troy — which became London. His name came to mean "hero" or "Briton" as a noun and "brave" as an adjective.

The *cause efficiat* is a term from Aristotle meaning the efficient cause; that is, it is the instrument that produced the effect. In this case the *cause efficiat* was the magic mirror.

Bacon used one of the boys' daggers to break the magic mirror, saying, "So vanishes the magic mirror, and the shows in the magic mirror that necromancy infused into the mirror end with it."

"Why does learned Bacon thus break his mirror?" Friar Bungay asked.

"I tell thee, Bungay, I strongly regret that Bacon ever meddled in this art. The hours I have spent in pyromantic spells, the fearful tossing in the latent night of papers full of necromantic charms, conjuring and banishing devils and fiends, with stole and alb and strange pentagram, the wresting and perverting of the holy name of God, as Sother, Eloïm, and Adonai, Alpha, Manoth, and Tetragrammaton, with praying to the five-fold powers of Heaven, are reasons that Bacon must be damned for using devils to counterbalance his God."

Bacon would summon demons and keep them out of Hell so that they could obey his orders.

Members of the clergy wore the stole and alb. The alb is a long white robe, while the stole is a long strip of cloth worn over the shoulders and hanging in front below the chest. Because demons dislike the clergy, wearing the stole and alb protected magicians.

Sother, Eloïm, and Adonai, Alpha, Manoth, and Tetragrammaton are all names for God. The Tetragrammaton is JHVH, or Jehovah. Friar Bacon had probably put a name of God on each of the five points of the pentagram. In addition, magicians would often take the name "Jehovah" and make anagrams of it.

God made the physical laws of the universe, but Bacon had summoned devils to counteract those laws, thus going against the will of God. In doing so, he had misused the names of God.

Friar Bacon continued, "Yet, Bacon, cheer up and don't drown in despair.

"Sins have their salves, and repentance can do much: Remember that Mercy sits where Justice holds her seat, and from those wounds that those bloody Jews did pierce, which by thy magic metaphorically often did bleed afresh, from thence for thee the dew of mercy drops, to wash away the wrath of high Jehovah's ire, and make thee as a new-born babe free from sin.

"Bungay, I'll spend the remnant of my life in pure devotion, praying to my God that He would save the soul that Bacon vainly and foolishly lost."

CHAPTER 14

— Scene 14 —

At Fressingfield, Margaret was wearing the habit of a nun in the presence of the gamekeeper and a friend. Margaret was preparing to take her vows as a nun.

"Margaret, be not so headstrong in these vows," the gamekeeper said. "Oh, don't bury such beauty in a cell — England has made you famous because of your beauty! Thy father's hair, which resembles the silver blooms that beautify the shrubs of Africa, shall fall out prematurely before their appointed time of death, if he were thus to lose his lovely Margaret."

His daughter, Margaret, replied, "Ah, father, when the harmony of Heaven sounds the music of a living faith, the vain illusions of this flattering world seem odious to the thoughts of Margaret.

"I loved once — Lord Lacy was my love. And now I hate myself for having loved and for having doted more on him than on my God — because of this I scourge — whip — myself with sharp repentance and penances. But now the blemish of such ambitious sins tells me that all love is lust except for the love of the Heavens; the blemish of such filled-with-desires sins also tells me that beauty used for love is vanity.

"The world contains nothing but alluring temptations, pride, flattery, and inconstant, fickle thoughts. To shun and avoid the pricks and stings of death, I leave the world and vow to meditate on Heavenly bliss and to live in Fremingham as a holy nun, holy and pure in conscience and in deed. And I vow this because I wish all maidens to learn from me to seek Heaven's joy before Earth's vanity."

"And will you, then, Margaret, be shorn a nun and initiated into the nunnery, and so leave us all?" the friend asked.

"Now farewell, world, the engine and means of all woe!" Margaret said. "Farewell to friends and father! Welcome, Christ! Adieu to dainty robes! This base attire better befits a mind that is humble before God than all the show of rich habiliments. Farewell, oh, love! And, along with foolish love, farewell to Sweet Lacy, whom I loved once so dearly! Always be well, but never be in my thoughts, lest I offend by thinking about Lacy's love. But even to that, as to the rest, farewell!"

Lacy, Warren, and Ermsby arrived. They were booted and spurred because they had been riding on horseback. Because of Lacy's hurry to find Margaret, they had not taken time to remove their spurs.

"Come on, my wags, we're near the gamekeeper's lodge," Lacy said. "Here I have often walked in the watery meadows and chatted with my lovely Margaret."

"Sirrah Ned, isn't this the gamekeeper I see?" Warren asked.

Lacy looked and said, "Yes, that's him."

"The old lecher has gotten holy mutton for himself: a nun, my lord," Ermsby said.

The word "mutton" was slang for "prostitute."

"Gamekeeper, how are thou?" Lacy asked. "Hello, man, what is thine mood? How is Peggy, thy daughter and my love?"

"Ah, my good lord!" the gamekeeper said. "Oh, I feel woe because of Peggy! See where she stands clad in her nun's attire, ready to be shorn and initiated into a religious life in Fremingham. She leaves the world because she left — lost — your love. Oh, my good lord, persuade her not to become a nun if you can!"

"Why, how are you now, Margaret!" Lacy said. "Unhappy? A nun! What holy father taught you to task yourself to such a tedious life and die an unmarried maiden! It would be an injury to me if you were to smother up such beauty in a cell."

Margaret replied, "Lord Lacy, thinking of my former sin, how foolishly the prime of my light-hearted years was spent in love — oh, shame upon that foolish notion called love, whose occurrence and essence hang upon the perception of the eye! — I leave both love and love's content at once, instead committing myself to Him Who is true love, and leaving all the world for love of Him."

"From where, Peggy, comes this metamorphosis?" Lacy said. "What! Shorn a nun, and I have from the court ridden swiftly with coursers to convey thee from here to Windsor, where our marriage shall be celebrated! Thy wedding-robes are in the tailor's hands. Come, Peggy, leave these peremptory vows."

"Didn't my lord — you — resign his interest in me, and make a divorce between Margaret and him?" she replied, using the third person.

"It was only to test sweet Peggy's constancy and faithfulness to me," Lacy said. "But will fair Margaret leave her love and lord?"

"Isn't Heaven's joy superior to Earth's fading, corrupting bliss, and isn't life above with God sweeter than life in love?"

"Why, then, Margaret, will you be shorn a nun?" Lacy asked.

Using the third person, she replied, "Margaret has made a vow that may not be revoked."

"We cannot stay, my lord, if she is so unrelenting," Warren said. "We don't have time for you to woo her anew."

They needed to ride back to the court to attend the wedding of Prince Edward and Princess Eleanor.

"Choose, fair damsel, the choice is still yours," Ermsby said. "Choose either a solemn nunnery or the court. Choose either God or Lord Lacy. Choose whichever will make you happiest: to be a nun or else Lord Lacy's wife?"

"A good proposal," Lacy said. "Well put!"

He then said, "Peggy, your answer must be quick."

Matthew 26:41 states, "*Watch, and pray, that ye enter not into temptation: the spirit indeed is ready, but the flesh is weak*" (1599 Geneva Bible).

Margaret said, "The flesh is frail ... my lord knows it well ... that when he comes to me with his enchanting face, whatever may happen, I cannot say him nay. Off goes the habit of a maiden's heart, and, seeing Lady Fortune's will for me, I say to fair Fremingham, and all the show of holy nuns, farewell! Lacy is for me, if he will be my lord."

"Peggy, I will be thy lord, thy love, thy husband," Lacy said. "Trust me. I swear by the truth of my knighthood that the king is waiting to marry matchless Eleanor to his son until I bring thee richly to the court, so that one and the same day may both marry her and thee."

He then asked, "What do thou say about this, gamekeeper? Are thou glad of this?"

"I am as glad as if the English king had given the park and deer of Fressingfield to me," the gamekeeper replied.

Seeing Warren, the Earl of Sussex, deep in thought, Ermsby said, "Please tell me, my Lord of Sussex, why are thou in a brown study. Why are you lost in serious thought?"

"Because I see the nature of women," Ermsby replied. "Be they never so near God, yet they love to die in a man's arms."

In this culture, "to die in a man's arms" meant "to have an orgasm in a man's arms."

"What have you prepared for breakfast?" Lacy asked Margaret. "We have hastened and ridden on horseback all this night to Fressingfield."

"Butter and cheese, and the organs of a deer, such as poor gamekeepers have within their lodge," Margaret answered.

"And not a bottle of wine?" Lacy asked.

"We'll find one for my lord," Margaret said.

"Come, Sussex, let us go in," Lacy said. "We shall have more, for she speaks least, to hold her promise sure."

He meant that they would have better food and drink than Margaret had mentioned because she had promised the least in order to make sure that she could keep her promise.

CHAPTER 15

A devil, seeking Miles, said to himself, "How restless are the ghosts of Hellish spirits, when every charmer — every sorcerer — with his magic spells calls us from the Phlegethon River, which circles Hell nine times, to hurry and sweep over the Earth quickly on the speedy wings of the swiftest winds! Now Bacon has raised me from the darkest deep to search the world for Miles, his servant, and to torment his lazy body for carelessly and negligently watching his Brazen Head and not informing him when the Head spoke.

"I see Miles coming now. Oh, he is mine."

Miles, dressed in an academic gown and a corner-cap, complained about being unable to find a job as a professor: "'A scholar!' said a prospective employer. 'Indeed, sir,' I replied. I wish I had been made a bottle-maker when I was made a scholar, for I can't get a job as a deacon, reader, or schoolmaster, no, or as the clerk of a parish."

A deacon is an assistant to a priest or pastor, a reader is someone who reads sermons in a church service, and a clerk of a parish is an administrative officer who assists the clergyman.

Miles continued, "Some called me a dunce; another said my head is as full of Latin as an egg is full of oatmeal."

In other words, he did not know Latin.

He continued, "Thus I am tormented, and thus the devil and Friar Bacon haunt me."

Seeing the devil, he said, "Good Lord, here's one of my master's devils! I'll go and speak to him."

He then asked the devil, "Master Plutus, how are you?"

Plutus is the god of wealth; Miles was confusing him with Pluto, the god of the underworld.

"Do thou know me?" the devil asked.

"Know you, sir! Why, aren't you one of my master's devils that were accustomed to come to my master, Doctor Bacon, at Brazen-nose?"

"Yes, indeed, I am," the devil said.

"Good Lord, Master Plutus, I have seen you a thousand times at my master's, and yet I had never the manners to offer you a drink. But, sir, I am glad to see how conformable you are to the statute."

England had sumptuary laws regulating who could wear sumptuous clothing. People were prohibited from wearing clothing of the sort that was worn by people above their social class.

Miles turned to you, the readers of this book, and said, "I promise you that he's as yeomanly a man as you shall see."

The devil was dressed like a yeoman — a small landowner.

Miles added, "See, gentlemen readers, here's a plain honest man, without welt or guard."

Miles forgot to mention the gentlewomen readers of this book. The author apologizes for him.

"Welt" and "guard" referred to fancy ornaments and trimming. This devil did not wear those.

Miles turned to the devil and said, "But I ask you, sir, have you come lately from Hell?"

"Yes, indeed," the devil replied, "What about it?"

"Indeed, it is a place I have long desired to see," Miles said. "Haven't you good tippling-houses — taverns — there? Mayn't a man have a vigorous fire there, a pot of good ale, a pack of cards, a large piece of chalk for recording tabs, and a piece of brown toast that will be dropped down on the white waistcoat of a cup of good drink?"

The "white waistcoat" is foam. In this culture, a piece of toast was put on top of a drink to act as a sop.

"All this you may have there," the devil said.

"You are for me, friend, and I am for you," Miles said. "But I ask you, mayn't I have a job there?"

"Yes, a thousand. What would thou be? What job do you want?"

"Truly, sir, I want a job in a place where I may profit and advance myself," Miles said. "I know Hell is a hot place, and men are marvelously dry, and much drink is spent there, and so I want to be a tapster — a bartender."

"Thou shall," the devil said.

"There's nothing that prevents me from going with you, except that it is a long journey, and I don't have a horse."

"Thou shall ride on my back," the devil said.

"Now surely here's a courteous devil, that, in order to pleasure his friend, will not hesitate to make a jade — a bad horse — of himself," Miles said. "But I ask you, goodman friend, to let me ask you a question."

A "goodman" is a man who ranks socially just below a gentleman.

"What is it?"

"Please, tell me whether your pace is a trot or an amble?"

An "amble" is a walk.

"An amble," the devil answered.

"That's fine; but take care it is not a trot," Miles said, "but that doesn't matter. I'll anticipate it so I can prevent it."

Miles started putting on spurs.

"What are you doing?" the devil asked.

"Indeed, I am putting on my spurs, for if I find your pace either a trot or else uneasy, I'll put you to a false gallop: I'll make you feel the benefit of my spurs."

A "false gallop" is a canter or easy gallop. It is faster than a trot but not as fast as a gallop.

"Get upon my back," the devil said.

"Oh, Lord, here's even a splendid marvel, when a man rides to Hell on the devil's back!"

Miles got on the devil's back and rode away. He and the devil made a noisy exit.

CHAPTER 16

— Scene 16 —

The double wedding had been performed, and at the court, a procession now took place in this order:

1. The Emperor of Germany entered, carrying a pointless sword that symbolized mercy.

2. The King of Castile entered, carrying a pointed sword that symbolized justice.

3. Lacy entered, carrying a golden globe that symbolized sovereignty and earthly power.

4. Prince Edward entered.

5. Warren entered, carrying a rod of gold with a dove on it. The rod of gold symbolized equity, fairness, and impartiality. The dove symbolized the sanctifying power of the Holy Spirit. If something is sanctified, it is set apart as being holy.

6. Ermsby entered, carrying a crown and a scepter.

7. Princess Eleanor, now married to Prince Edward, entered.

8. Margaret, now the Countess of Lincoln, entered on Princess Eleanor's left hand.

9. King Henry III of England entered.

10. Friar Bacon entered.

11. Attending Lords entered.

Prince Edward said, "Great potentates, Earth's miracles with respect to authority, understand that Prince Edward humbles himself and kneels at your feet, and for these favors you have shown, on his martial sword he vows perpetual homage to yourselves for yielding these honors to Eleanor."

"Great thanks, lordings," King Henry III said. "Old Plantagenet — me — who rules and sways the Albion diadem — the English crown — with tears manifests these apprehended joys, and vows to repay you, if his men-at-arms, the wealth of England, or due honors done to Eleanor may repay his favorites."

His favorites were also his favorers.

He turned to the Emperor of Germany and asked, "But all this while what do you say to the dames who shine like the crystal lamps — the stars — of Heaven?"

The dames were Eleanor and Margaret.

The Emperor of Germany replied, "If but a third beauty were added to these two, they would surpass those gorgeous images who gloried Ida with rich beauty's wealth."

On Mount Ida, three beautiful goddesses — Hera, Athena, and Aphrodite — competed in a beauty contest judged by Prince Paris of Troy. Add a third beauty to Eleanor and Margaret, and the beauty of the three mortals would surpass the beauty of the three goddesses. The three goddesses' Roman names are Juno, Minerva, and Venus.

"It is I, my lords, who humbly on my knee must yield her prayers to mighty Jove — God — for lifting up and raising his handmaid to this state and social rank," Margaret said. "She — I — was brought from her humble cottage to the court, and honored by kings, princes, and emperors, to whom (second only to the noble Lincoln Earl, my husband) I vow obedience, and such humble love as a handmaid may give to such mighty men."

Eleanor said, "Thou martial man who wears the Almain — German — crown, and you the western potentates of might, the Albion princess, English Edward's wife — me — is proud that the lovely star of Fressingfield, beautiful Margaret, Countess to the Lincoln Earl, attends on Eleanor."

Margaret was now one of Princess Eleanor's ladies-in-waiting. This was a high honor for Margaret.

Eleanor continued, "I give great thanks, Lord Lacy, for Margaret. It is I who give thanks to you all for Margaret, and I am remain obliged to all of you for her worthy self."

King Henry III said, "Seeing the marriage is solemnized, let's march in triumph to the royal feast.

"But why does Friar Bacon stand here so mute?"

"I am repentant for the follies of my youth, whom magic's secret mysteries misled," Friar Bacon said, "and I am joyful that this royal marriage is an omen of such bliss to this unparalleled realm."

"Why, Bacon, what strange event shall happen to this land?" King Henry III asked. "Or what shall grow from Edward and his queen?"

Friar Bacon now foretold the coming of the great Queen Elizabeth I of England. In 1254, Prince Edward married Eleanor of Castile. Elizabeth was born in 1558. Queen Elizabeth was a direct descendant of King Henry III.

Friar Bacon said, "I find by deep prescience and foreseeing of my magical art, which once I honed in my secret cell, that here where Brutus did build his Troynovant, from forth the royal garden of a king [Henry VIII] shall flourish out so rich and fair a bud [Elizabeth I], whose brightness shall outshine the beauty of proud Phoebus' flower, and cast a protective shadow over Albion with her leaves."

Phoebus Apollo's flower is the hyacinth, which came into existence after the youth named Hyacinthus, whom Apollo loved, died.

Friar Bacon continued, "Until then Mars, god of war, shall be master of the battlefield, but then the stormy threats of wars shall cease. The horse shall stamp its hooves without fear of the weapon called the pike, and drums shall be turned to timbrels — tambourines — of delight.

"With wealthy favors aplenty she [Elizabeth I] shall enrich the shore and land that wandering Brutus — the descendant of Aeneas and the first King of England — was glad to see, and peace from Heaven shall harbor in these gorgeous leaves that beautify this matchless flower.

"Apollo's heliotrope then shall bow down, and Venus' hyacinth shall vail her top. Juno shall shut her gilliflowers up, and Pallas Athena's bay tree shall be abashed despite its brightest green. Ceres' carnation, in company with those other flowers, shall stoop and wonder at Diana's rose."

A heliotrope is a flower that always faces the sun during the day. Ships vailed their tops — that is, lowered their topsail — as a sign of respect to another ship.

Metaphorically, Diana's rose is Elizabeth. Diana was a virgin goddess, and Elizabeth was a virgin queen.

King Henry III said, "This prophecy is mystical and allegorical.

"But, glorious commanders who serve Europa's Love — Jupiter, aka God — Who makes fair England like that wealthy isle — the Garden of Eden — that is encircled with the Gihon and swift Euphrates rivers, in royalizing Henry's Albion with the presence of your princely mightiness, let's march.

"The tables all are set, and food such as England's wealth provides is ready to be set on the tables. You shall have a welcome, mighty potentates.

"To finish the preparations for this royal feast, let your hearts be only frolicsome; for the time requires that we taste of nothing but joy.

"Thus glories England over all the west."

***

Omne tulit punctum qui miscuit utile dulci.
This is a Latin quotation from Horace's *De Arta Poetica* (*Poetic Art*), verse 343.

As translated by C. Smart: *He who joins the instructive with the agreeable, carries off every vote, by delighting and at the same time admonishing the reader.*

In other words: Someone who combines education and entertainment earns praise.

APPENDIX A: NOTES

Scene 1

Ralph the Jester

Jesters go way back in history, including the time of the Persian Caliph Haroun-al-Rashid, who is in the *Arabian Nights*. When the Caliph got married, he ordered his jester, the dwarf Bahalul, to commit the most heinous crime possible. In addition, he ordered Bahalul to then justify his crime with an even more heinous excuse. Bahalul pretended to be downcast and left the room, but later he returned, snuck behind the Caliph and goosed his butt. He then "excused" his crime by saying, "Pardon me, my lord, your behind is so round and plumb I thought I was goosing the queen." Although Bahalul had followed the Caliph's orders, he was ordered to never set food on Persian soil again. Bahalul left for a while, but then he returned. The Caliph asked him, "Didn't I forbid you ever to set foot on Persian soil?" Bahalul replied, "You did, and I have followed your majesty's orders." He then took off one of his shoes and showed that it had Egyptian soil inside.

Source: Retold in my own words from this book:

Daniel P Mannix, *Freaks: We Who Are Not As Others*. Pp. 38-39.

Scene 2

"Brazen-nose"

Here is an excerpt from "The oddest name in Oxford":

The name of the College [Brasenose College] has always fascinated visitors to Oxford. There have been several interpretations of it, including the suggestion that it is derived from 'brasen huis' (brew house). The most likely explanation is that it refers to a 'brazen' (brass or bronze) door knocker in the shape of a nose.

Source: "The oddest name in Oxford." Brazenose College, University of Oxford. Accessed 10 December 2018.

Scene 8

Aspasia

This is an except from Plutarch's "Life of Artaxerxes":

3 Now, there was a custom among the Persians that the one appointed to the royal succession should ask a boon, and that the one who appointed him should give whatever was asked, if it was within his power. Accordingly, Dareius asked for

Aspasia, who had been the special favourite of Cyrus, and was then a concubine of the king. She was a native of Phocaea, in Ionia, born of free parents, and fittingly educated.

4 Once when Cyrus was at supper she was led in to him along with other women. The rest of the women took the seats given them, and when Cyrus proceeded to sport and dally and jest with them, showed no displeasure at his friendly advances. But Aspasia stood by her couch in silence, and would not obey when Cyrus called her; and when his chamberlains would have her led to him, she said: "Verily, whosoever lays his hands upon me shall rue the day." The guests therefore thought her a graceless and rude creature.

5 But Cyrus was delighted, and laughed, and said to the man who had brought the women: "Dost thou not see at once that this is the only free and unperverted woman thou hast brought me?" From this time on he was devoted to her, and loved her above all women, and called her The Wise. She was taken prisoner when Cyrus fell in the battle at Cunaxa and his camp was plundered.

Source: Plutarch, "The Life of Artaxerxes." *The Parallel Lives by Plutarch.* Published in Vol. XI of the Loeb Classical Library edition, 1926.

Scene 10

For I will straight to stately Fremingham,
And in the abbey there be shorn a nun,

Below is some interesting information on the shorning of a present-day nun:

Are the heads of new Catholic Nuns shaved?

Not any more in any of the traditional monastic Orders or any of the active Congregations in the Western Hemisphere, as far as I know.

When we received the habit in the very traditional Order to which I belonged, the ceremony called for "cutting the hair in the form of a cross". Until the Mistress of Novices explained it to me, I was all nerves, wondering what they were going to do to me! In the event, it turned out to be symbolic, like so many of the ancient practices that are still honored in our day. It only meant that as I bowed my head prior to receiving the veil the abbess took a pair of sewing shears (yikes!) and lifted up a lock of my hair and cut it off close to the scalp. She did this four times, choosing locks from the front, back, left, and right sides of the crown of my head, laying each shorn lock into a silver tray that was held by another senior nun.

Now, it is true that we were allowed to do pretty much what we wanted with our hair, once we were in habit. Most of my sisters simply kept it short in a kind of pixie cut [...].

Another of the younger nuns and I preferred a shaved head under the heavy veil, so every now and then we shaved each other's head. That was entirely our own desire, not a rule. Frankly, we had more important things on our minds.

Source: Claire-Edith de la Croix, Catholic sister. Jewish convert via Evangelicalism. "Are the heads of new Catholic Nuns shaved?" Quora. 6 October 2017.

Scene 16

Omne tulit punctum qui miscuit utile dulci.

This is a quotation from Horace's *De Arta Poetica* (*Poetic Art*), verse 343.

Here is a pubic domain translation from Tufts University's Perseus Project:

He who joins the instructive with the agreeable, carries off every vote, by delighting and at the same time admonishing the reader.

Source:

Q. Horatius Flaccus (Horace), *The Art of Poetry: To the Pisos*. C. Smart, Theodore Alois Buckley, Ed.

APPENDIX B: ABOUT THE AUTHOR

It was a dark and stormy night. Suddenly a cry rang out, and on a hot summer night in 1954, Josephine, wife of Carl Bruce, gave birth to a boy — me. Unfortunately, this young married couple allowed Reuben Saturday, Josephine's brother, to name their first-born. Reuben, aka "The Joker," decided that Bruce was a nice name, so he decided to name me Bruce Bruce. I have gone by my middle name — David — ever since.

Being named Bruce David Bruce hasn't been all bad. Bank tellers remember me very quickly, so I don't often have to show an ID. It can be fun in charades, also. When I was a counselor as a teenager at Camp Echoing Hills in Warsaw, Ohio, a fellow counselor gave the signs for "sounds like" and "two words," then she pointed to a bruise on her leg twice. Bruise Bruise? Oh yeah, Bruce Bruce is the answer!

Uncle Reuben, by the way, gave me a haircut when I was in kindergarten. He cut my hair short and shaved a small bald spot on the back of my head. My mother wouldn't let me go to school until the bald spot grew out again.

Of all my brothers and sisters (six in all), I am the only transplant to Athens, Ohio. I was born in Newark, Ohio, and have lived all around Southeastern Ohio. However, I moved to Athens to go to Ohio University and have never left.

At Ohio U, I never could make up my mind whether to major in English or Philosophy, so I got a Bachelor's with a double major in both areas in 1980, then I added a Master's in English in 1984 and a Master's in Philosophy in 1985. Currently, I am a retired English instructor at Ohio U.

If all goes well, I will publish one or two books a year for the rest of my life. (On the other hand, a good way to make God laugh is to tell Her your plans.)

By the way, my sister Brenda Kennedy writes romances such as *A New Beginning* and *Shattered Dreams*.

APPENDIX C: SOME BOOKS BY DAVID BRUCE

Retellings of a Classic Work of Literature

Arden of Faversham: *A Retelling*

Ben Jonson's The Alchemist: *A Retelling*

Ben Jonson's The Arraignment, or Poetaster: *A Retelling*

Ben Jonson's Bartholomew Fair: *A Retelling*

Ben Jonson's The Case is Altered: *A Retelling*

Ben Jonson's Catiline's Conspiracy: *A Retelling*

Ben Jonson's The Devil is an Ass: *A Retelling*

Ben Jonson's Epicene: *A Retelling*

Ben Jonson's Every Man in His Humor: *A Retelling*

Ben Jonson's Every Man Out of His Humor: *A Retelling*

Ben Jonson's The Fountain of Self-Love, or Cynthia's Revels: *A Retelling*

Ben Jonson's The Magnetic Lady, or Humors Reconciled: *A Retelling*

Ben Jonson's The New Inn, or The Light Heart: *A Retelling*

Ben Jonson's Sejanus' Fall: *A Retelling*

Ben Jonson's The Staple of News: *A Retelling*

Ben Jonson's A Tale of a Tub: *A Retelling*

Ben Jonson's Volpone, or the Fox: *A Retelling*

Christopher Marlowe's Complete Plays: Retellings

Christopher Marlowe's Dido, Queen of Carthage: *A Retelling*

Christopher Marlowe's Doctor Faustus: *Retellings of the 1604 A-Text and of the 1616 B-Text*

Christopher Marlowe's Edward II: *A Retelling*

Christopher Marlowe's The Massacre at Paris: *A Retelling*

Christopher Marlowe's The Rich Jew of Malta: *A Retelling*

Christopher Marlowe's Tamburlaine, Parts 1 and 2: *Retellings*

Dante's Divine Comedy: *A Retelling in Prose*

Dante's Inferno: *A Retelling in Prose*

Dante's Purgatory: *A Retelling in Prose*

Dante's Paradise: *A Retelling in Prose*

The Famous Victories of Henry V: *A Retelling*

From the Iliad *to the* Odyssey: *A Retelling in Prose of Quintus of Smyrna's* Posthomerica

George Chapman, Ben Jonson, and John Marston's Eastward Ho! *A Retelling*

George Peele's The Arraignment of Paris: *A Retelling*

George Peele's The Battle of Alcazar: *A Retelling*

George Peele's David and Bathsheba, and the Tragedy of Absalom: *A Retelling*

George Peele's Edward I: *A Retelling*

George Peele's The Old Wives' Tale: *A Retelling*

George-a-Greene: *A Retelling*

The History of King Leir: A Retelling

Homer's Iliad: *A Retelling in Prose*

Homer's Odyssey: *A Retelling in Prose*

J.W. Gent.'s The Valiant Scot: *A Retelling*

Jason and the Argonauts: A Retelling in Prose of Apollonius of Rhodes' Argonautica

John Ford: Eight Plays Translated into Modern English

John Ford's The Broken Heart: *A Retelling*

John Ford's The Fancies, Chaste and Noble: *A Retelling*

John Ford's The Lady's Trial: *A Retelling*

John Ford's The Lover's Melancholy: *A Retelling*

John Ford's Love's Sacrifice: *A Retelling*

John Ford's Perkin Warbeck: *A Retelling*

John Ford's The Queen: *A Retelling*

John Ford's 'Tis Pity She's a Whore: *A Retelling*

John Lyly's Campaspe: *A Retelling*

John Lyly's Endymion, The Man in the Moon: *A Retelling*

John Lyly's Galatea: *A Retelling*

John Lyly's Love's Metamorphosis: *A Retelling*

John Lyly's Midas: *A Retelling*

John Lyly's Mother Bombie: *A Retelling*

John Lyly's Sappho and Phao: *A Retelling*

John Lyly's The Woman in the Moon: *A Retelling*

John Webster's The White Devil: *A Retelling*

King Edward III: *A Retelling*

Mankind: *A Medieval Morality Play* (A Retelling)

Margaret Cavendish's The Unnatural Tragedy: *A Retelling*

The Merry Devil of Edmonton: *A Retelling*

The Summoning of Everyman: *A Medieval Morality Play* (A Retelling)

Robert Greene's Friar Bacon and Friar Bungay: *A Retelling*

The Taming of a Shrew: *A Retelling*

Tarlton's Jests: A Retelling

Thomas Middleton's A Chaste Maid in Cheapside: *A Retelling*

Thomas Middleton's Women Beware Women: *A Retelling*

Thomas Middleton and Thomas Dekker's The Roaring Girl: *A Retelling*

Thomas Middleton and William Rowley's The Changeling: *A Retelling*

The Trojan War and Its Aftermath: Four Ancient Epic Poems

Virgil's Aeneid: *A Retelling in Prose*

William Shakespeare's 5 Late Romances: Retellings in Prose

William Shakespeare's 10 Histories: Retellings in Prose

William Shakespeare's 11 Tragedies: Retellings in Prose

William Shakespeare's 12 Comedies: Retellings in Prose

William Shakespeare's 38 Plays: Retellings in Prose

William Shakespeare's 1 Henry IV, aka Henry IV, Part 1: *A Retelling in Prose*

William Shakespeare's 2 Henry IV, aka Henry IV, Part 2: *A Retelling in Prose*

William Shakespeare's 1 Henry VI, aka Henry VI, Part 1: *A Retelling in Prose*

William Shakespeare's 2 Henry VI, aka Henry VI, Part 2: *A Retelling in Prose*

William Shakespeare's 3 Henry VI, aka Henry VI, Part 3: *A Retelling in Prose*

William Shakespeare's All's Well that Ends Well: *A Retelling in Prose*

William Shakespeare's Antony and Cleopatra: *A Retelling in Prose*

William Shakespeare's As You Like It: *A Retelling in Prose*

William Shakespeare's The Comedy of Errors: *A Retelling in Prose*

William Shakespeare's Coriolanus: *A Retelling in Prose*

William Shakespeare's Cymbeline: *A Retelling in Prose*

William Shakespeare's Hamlet: *A Retelling in Prose*

William Shakespeare's Henry V: *A Retelling in Prose*

William Shakespeare's Henry VIII: *A Retelling in Prose*

William Shakespeare's Julius Caesar: *A Retelling in Prose*

William Shakespeare's King John: *A Retelling in Prose*

William Shakespeare's King Lear: *A Retelling in Prose*

William Shakespeare's Love's Labor's Lost: *A Retelling in Prose*

William Shakespeare's Macbeth: *A Retelling in Prose*

William Shakespeare's Measure for Measure: *A Retelling in Prose*

William Shakespeare's The Merchant of Venice: *A Retelling in Prose*

William Shakespeare's The Merry Wives of Windsor: *A Retelling in Prose*

William Shakespeare's A Midsummer Night's Dream: *A Retelling in Prose*

William Shakespeare's Much Ado About Nothing: *A Retelling in Prose*

William Shakespeare's Othello: *A Retelling in Prose*

William Shakespeare's Pericles, Prince of Tyre: *A Retelling in Prose*

William Shakespeare's Richard II: *A Retelling in Prose*

William Shakespeare's Richard III: *A Retelling in Prose*

William Shakespeare's Romeo and Juliet: *A Retelling in Prose*

William Shakespeare's The Taming of the Shrew: *A Retelling in Prose*

William Shakespeare's The Tempest: *A Retelling in Prose*

William Shakespeare's Timon of Athens: *A Retelling in Prose*

William Shakespeare's Titus Andronicus: *A Retelling in Prose*

William Shakespeare's Troilus and Cressida: *A Retelling in Prose*

William Shakespeare's Twelfth Night: *A Retelling in Prose*

William Shakespeare's The Two Gentlemen of Verona: *A Retelling in Prose*

William Shakespeare's The Two Noble Kinsmen: *A Retelling in Prose*

William Shakespeare's The Winter's Tale: *A Retelling in Prose*